ONE GOOD MAN

A Gay Marine Corps Novel

by Derek Pace

Printed in the United States of America

ISBN: 978-1546393719

This is a work of fiction. All of the characters, names, incidents, organizations, and dialogue in this novel are either the products of the author's imagination or are used fictitiously.

Acknowledgements:

I'd like to thank Isaac for being my Beta reader, Next_Hub for the the cover, and most of all, Alex for pushing me to write this.

Dedicated to Alex, for convincing me to push my boundaries.

TABLE OF CONTENTS

Chapter 1: Doing What Marines Do

My nerves were on high alert as we patrolled down the dusty Fallujah street. This wasn't 2004 when the Marines fought the largest battle in a built-up area on these same streets since WWII, and it wasn't Ramadi where the Fallujah mujahedeen had fled after the battle, but still, it could be hairy out on patrol—and I got off on it. There's something to be said about the rush of adrenaline that surges through your body when going outside the wire. It's as if every brain cell is alive and working on overdrive.

I am Corporal Alexander Harkin Indigo, USMC. I'm an 0301, a grunt. An infantryman. A fire team leader with Bravo Company, First Battalion, First Marines, the "First of the First," and deployed to Camp Fallujah, Iraq.

I scanned up high as the patrol moved down the dusty street. The muj had a habit of using the roofs, either to fire on us or to tell someone else that we were coming. Someone simply watching us was not within our ROE, or Rules of Engagement, to take him out, but if he got on a cell, at least we could light it up around him, convincing him that what he was doing wasn't conducive to a long and happy life.

We weren't out in the middle of Fallujah alone. The entire platoon was on patrol, each squad in a stack. That way, the platoon could cover more ground, but each squad could support each other if it came to that.

The day was hot, no surprise, and the sweat was pouring down my face despite the field scarf I had wrapped around my forehead under my helmet. I could pull it down over my mouth if the dust got kicked up too bad, but for now, I was using it to soak up what sweat it could.

We were on a simple show-our-face patrol, reminding the muj that we were around. We'd be back before evening chow, but still, we were loaded for bear with 75 lbs of gear and ammo. So far, the platoon had been lucky during the deployment, with only two injuries, and those from the weight we hauled on our backs, not enemy action. That was probably pretty good, considering.

Usually, we carried much more weight, and the wear and tear were pretty serious. Muscular-skeletal injuries were common, and I figured the VA would be having its hands full with claims as the years went on. These issues would be the Iraq and the Afghanistan wars' Agent Orange.

Up ahead, the squad's point man, PFC Whitman, held up a clenched fist, the signal to halt. I held up my fist and took a knee, adjusting the straps of my pack where it was cutting into my shoulders. Sergeant Jackson, our squad leader, moved forward. I ignored him, keeping my eyes peeled. He'd let us know if there was going to be a change in our orders.

On the second floor across the street, I saw movement, and I brought up my M16A4. A woman was edging forward to where she could see us. It was probably curiosity, but there were female muj as well, so I signaled to Lance Corporal Chester Leister, my AR-man, to keep his eyes on her. I could count on the fact that Chester the Molester would light her up if she even moved funny.

"Fire team leaders up!" the call came down the line.

With only a slight creaking in my knees, I stood and moved forward to where Sergeant Jackson was waiting with Ben La Rosa, the Second Fire Team leader. A moment later, B-Man joined us.

It wasn't really a good idea for us to group up like that. The week before, an Army squad lost five soldiers when a mortar landed in the middle of a meeting like this. But we didn't have much choice if the sergeant needed to brief us.

"We've got a blood trail going into that building," Sergeant Jackson told us. "The lieutenant said one of the snipers hit a mujahedeen half an hour ago, and that's probably our boy. So, we're going in after him, and we want this guy alive if possible, so don't go in guns ablazing. Second Squad's going to move in to provide security and to cut off egress.

"OK, we've done this a million times. Nothing new here. We've maybe got a wounded or dead insurgent inside. We don't know who else might be there. Heads up, and think, think, think! Alex, you're the assault team. You're in first, and you clear to the left. B-Man, you're support. I want you in on Second Team's heels. Split the stack and clear to the right. Ben, make sure the bottom floor is cleared, then keep it secure. We don't need anyone coming up our asses from outside. After that, use our footholds and just talk it out. If we take a casualty, be ready to flood the house or break contact on my order. There's no room for mistakes here. Remember, 'tactical patience!'"

The "book" pushed for a top-down assault, that is, going in on the roof and working our way down a building. This tended to limit the egress routes the guerillas used to make their getaway and were easier to cover by the support element, and we could use grenades by throwing them down instead of up. For the martyr types, the insurgents who didn't expect to live but who wanted to take out as many of us as possible, they tended to barricade themselves in rooms and stairwells, and coming down at them was easier than fighting up.

We were pretty much stuck here, though, coming in on the ground floor and working our way up. Top down or bottom up, clearing a building was one of the more harrowing things we had to do in Iraq. The idea that right behind a door was a machine gun ready to take you out was always on your mind. Out in the street, there was a sense of distance, and even if they shot at you, there was room to maneuver. But in some small bedroom, not even an Iraqi could miss. The first guy into a room was at serious risk of getting taken out. This was ass-puckering territory.

"Doc, we know the guy's hurt, so go with Second. Do what you can do to keep him alive until we can turn him over to the ITT team.

"So, let's get ready. As soon as we get the OK from the lieutenant, we're going in."

Like many of the buildings in the city, this one had a wall in front protecting a courtyard. And like many buildings, it had been damaged, probably during the Battle for Fallujah in '04. There was a gaping hole in the wall that someone had tried to block off with strips of woven plastic. Scarlett blood on the white strips was bright in the sunlight, proof that someone had gone inside, and very recently. I was surprised that we hadn't seen him while we moved up the street.

I got my team up alongside the wall while we waited for Second Squad to move into position. I eyeballed the plastic strips, looking for telltale wires of a boobytrap. It looked clear, and I doubted that a wounded muj with a Marine patrol coming down on his ass would take the time to set one up.

Finally, the lieutenant gave us the OK, and it was go-time. We rushed through the opening, bypassing the gate, and up to the front door. Jesse, my Assistant AR-man, ran his hands along the jamb, looking for any sign of a boobytrap. He reached the knob and twisted, but it didn't move. It was locked. There went the first part of our subdued entry. I wondered for a moment if I should change to a dynamic entry, with us yelling and firing, tossing grenades as we went. But then again, if we were trying to capture someone, that probably wasn't the best way to go about it, unless we just wanted to recover a bullet-riddled corpse.

The Marines Corps had a hundred ways to breach a door, some of them pretty high tech. But for a rifle squad, it usually boiled down to the Mark 1 Mod 1 combat boot, a hooligan, or shooting out the lock with a shotgun or M16. An M203 was effective, but friendlies had to be pretty far back before one was used. SMAWs worked great, too, but a squad didn't always have access to one, and the same problem about standoff distance was there. We also carried an "eight ball," which was a 1/8 stick of C4, but the the issue of us having to get out of the blast zone made this less than the preferred course of action.

Jesse looked back at me, and I pointed over my shoulder as if I had something slung there. Jesse nodded, shouldered his M16, and unlimbered his Mossberg, and holding the muzzle down at an angle and touching the locking mechanism, sent one of the big Lockbuster-C slugs into the door. The door didn't have a chance and flopped open.

Immediately, we rushed in, just as we've practiced hundreds of times back at Pendleton and the Stumps. Of course, back in the States, we didn't have someone trying to kill us, and I was hyped as I burst through the door and juked to the left. First Team was right on our asses, breaking off to the right.

The bottom floor was empty. Like most Iraqi houses, the front door led to a small entry with two small sitting rooms alongside it. Two interior doors led to other rooms with a main hallway running to the back of the building. These interior doors could almost always be just kicked in, and Jesse had already breached one of them. There was a stairway going up to the left, and a quick glance showed me blood going up them.

Logic would have it that our target had gone up the stairs, but we couldn't just go up without the bottom floor cleared. Just because I saw the blood didn't mean that someone else wasn't downstairs ready to hit us, or even if the wounded muj hadn't doubled back.

I put Chester with his SAW and my newbie, PFC Warden Sung, at the stairwell, weapons pointing up.

"Coming in!" Quinton Chase shouted as Third Fire Team entered the building. With them clearing the bottom floor, we were free to start moving upstairs.

"Clear!" shouted Jesse to the left.

"Hold left, clear right!" I shouted out, letting Ben know to hold up until B-Man cleared their sector.

The shouts of "Next man in left," "Coming out," "Clear," "Move," and such were an ongoing newsfeed of how things were progressing. In just a few minutes, the shout of "All clear!" let me know that the bottom floor was secure. I turned to look at Sergeant Jackson, pointing up the ladderwell.

Going up stairwells was one of the diciest parts of clearing a building. The passageway was restricted, and anything could come tumbling down on you. Sergeant Jackson gave me the signal to move out. The four of us, with B-Man's team behind, started our well-rehearsed choreographed movement up the stairs, each move designed to keep the entire area covered. We could leave no area uncovered that would put us in danger. Despite being loaded down with a full combat load, it was almost a ballet.

I hugged the outside wall, my M16 with the M203 grenade launcher at the ready, eyes and ears searching for a grenade being dropped down the stairs. We made it to the next floor without incident and faced a long hallway. We split the stack again, with us clearing the rooms on the right, First Team the rooms on the left.

We found our wounded muj in the first room to the right.

Chester and Sung entered the first room, Chester immediately calling out, "Here he is!"

Jesse and I had gone into the second room, but upon hearing Chester, we ran back to the first room, with Doc Possum following us. The room was about 15 by 10, large for a room in an Iraqi house, and the furniture was surprisingly nice. The bed looked to be an antique, somehow surviving a century of war. Up against the side wall near the back was a small wardrobe that had seen better days. On the floor, up against the far wall under the window, was an older man, his shoulder a bloody mess. His white cotton shirt was stained crimson. He looked like he had been trying to reach the window, but his body had just given out. He was panting and looking up to us, an almost feral expression of a trapped animal in his face. I felt more than saw Doc try to move past me, and I stuck out my arm across his chest, stopping him.

He looked at me for a moment with a confused expression, but as Sung started to search the man, understanding flowed across his face. More than a few Marines had been killed by wounded men who'd chosen suicide rather than capture.

"We clear?" I asked, and Chester nodded.

I let Doc go forward. I watched for a moment as Doc started to administer to him. The guy winced as Doc touched his shoulder, but he didn't make a sound. I could see that our sniper had destroyed most of the shoulder. Even a cursory glance made it clear that the arm would never work again would probably have to come off. The arm below the mess of his shoulder stood in stark contrast to the hamburger of a joint. Aside from a stream of blood that had run down it, the lower arm and hand were clean. There wasn't even any dirt under his fingernails. I had figured that if he was shot, he must have been emplacing an IED or something, but this man hadn't been digging anything.

"He's going to make it," Doc told Sergeant Jackson who'd just come into the room.

"OK, well, patch him up, and we'll get him out of here.

"Leave two with Doc," he told me, "then we still need to clear the rest of the building."

With that he stepped out, joining the rest of the squad.

"Chester, get away from that window," I said. "You looking to become a target? Come, on with me. Jesse, you and Sung stay here with Doc."

The words were no sooner out of my mouth when the door to the wardrobe flew open, and a shape burst out, knocking Chester flat. I was barely aware of what was happening, but I reacted by instinct. I raised my M16A4 and fired a three-round burst into the man's center-mass as he raised an old pistol to aim at the prone Marine.

His black shirt exploded as the rounds hit, and he dropped like a rock, the pistol bouncing off the wooden floor.

"What the fuck, Chester! You didn't clear that thing!" I shouted.

"Coming in!" Sergeant Jackson shouted out as he rushed back into the room.

I was livid. This was a fucking boot mistake, not that of a seasoned lance corporal.

"What's your fifth step of room clearing?" I shouted, punching the slack-jawed Sung in the shoulder.

"Search the room," he and Chester answered in unison.

"That's right! Search the fucking room!"

"I . . . I . . . I don't know what happened. I searched the muj," Chester said, getting up off the floor, staring at the dead insurgent.

I waited for Sergeant Jackson to chew my ass, but he stood silently for a moment, then simply said, "Clear this room, then get on with the rest of them."

"You heard the man," I said. "Check out that damned wardrobe, under the bed, and everywhere else."

I stood there, still fuming. They knew better than that, but they let finding the wounded muj make them forget procedure. That almost cost Chester his life. A fucking insurgent hiding in a closet had almost killed him.

I looked at the crumbled body as Sung checked his pockets, and it suddenly hit me. I'd just killed a man. I'd been in firefights before, and I'd fired my weapon. But I hadn't actually killed another human being, at least that I knew. This was different. From five feet away, I had taken a human life.

People are not supposed to enjoy killing others. It's not civilized, right? But I felt more than excited. I felt . . . proud? Exhilarated?

This is what I'd been trained to do, and I'd reacted without thinking.

The new commanding general of I MEF, our overall commander, Lieutenant General Mad Dog Mattis, once said, "The first time you blow someone away is not an insignificant event. That said, there are some assholes in the world that just need to be shot."

As I looked at the dead muj, blood pooling from under him and spreading across the floor, I think I knew what he meant.

Chapter 2: I Don't Fuck Marines

I don't fuck Marines.

It's not that I don't like Marines. I am one after all, and I'm as gung-ho as they come. I plan on making the Marines my career, just like my dad and my grandfather. My dad recently retired as a master guns, and my grandfather made sergeant major, so you can say I bleed Marine Corps green.

So why don't I fuck Marines? I mean, as a whole, they look great, as I'm reminded right now as I looked around the weight room. Keeping fit is a religion in the Corps. But I'm like the diabetic kid in a candy store. I'm surrounded by all sorts of delectables, but I can't take a bite—or lick.

There are several reasons for this. The first is that I'm an alpha, a bull, a top, a dom. It's just the way I am. I take charge and have things my way. I control my relationships. Most Marines, gay, straight, or bi, are the same. We joined the Marines instead of the other services because we wanted to be part of the best. As a group, we're drawn from the most aggressive of the species. For another Marine and me to hook up, it would probably be like two bull moose, locking antlers, but instead of fighting for some cow, we're fighting for dominance over each other. That might not be bad for a one-night stand, but it's a recipe for disaster for a relationship.

More importantly, though, is the fact that these are my brothers, and incest isn't cool. I've fought with these guys, some of them through two tours in the Sandbox. There are bonds that are stronger than any hook-ups, and nothing is worth jeopardizing them. Even if I were straight and we had women in the infantry, I wouldn't touch them.

Then there's the practical aspect. DADT has been emplaced for 12 years now, and while it was supposed to keep gays and lesbians from being harassed and shit, it does not mean that we can openly serve. We have to stay in the closet. I've got parts of DADT memorized. If we "demonstrate a propensity or intent to engage in homosexual acts," we can't serve because our mere presence "would create an unacceptable risk to the high standards of morale, good order and discipline, and unit cohesion that are the essence of military capability."

That's some stupid shit, huh? It sucks, and I hate it. But I love the Corps, so I play the game.

"Hey, Alex, are you going to spot me?" Doc asked me, "Or are you just going to sit around with your thumb up your ass?"

Doc Possum was HM3 Eric Poussey, the squad corpsman, and the strongest member of the platoon, if not the company. I'd been daydreaming while he put his Mickey Mouse towel on the bench. The ratty towel did little to protect his back from the rest of our sweat, but if anyone outside the squad thought it was weird for a combat corpsman to have such a kid's towel, no one outside the squad thought it worth mentioning once they saw Doc Possum's bulk. Within the squad, though, we continually gave him a ration of shit. Brothers could do that.

I got behind him, flexing my legs slightly, my hands held palm up under the bar. Doc was benching 405 pounds, and I had to be ready in case he needed help. Four hundred pounds crashing down on an exposed neck could kill someone, and the Al Qaeda ragheads out there didn't need any help.

Doc doesn't like for anyone to help him lift the bar off the cradle. With a grunt, he raised it, then brought the bar down to his chest before pushing it back up. He managed six reps on his own, and I barely had to help him on the seventh, his breath exploding onto my crotch as he put everything into the last lift.

I'd long ago put the fact out of my mind that when I'm spotting someone on the bench, my dick was about six inches from the lifter's head. I'd been to a few gay gyms before, and there's a good bit of grab ass going on in them, and at one of those gyms, it was a running prank to plop a dick on a face when the guy was lifting heavy, but like I said, these were my brothers.

"Good job, Doc," I said. "You're a beast."

I helped B-Man take off four of the 45-lb plates, bringing the bar to a more manageable 225. Doc wiped the bench with Mickey and took his place behind the bench to spot.

Sometimes, as I looked around Camp Fallujah, it was hard to believe that we were in a combat zone despite the outgoing arty and the occasional incoming. This was nothing like Camp Falcon near Al-Mahmoudiyah, where we were deployed two years ago. We had hard racks, a mini-exchange, great chow, and this gym. Marines would make a gym out of gas cans and sand if they had to, but the equipment here was as good as anything back in the States. The building itself sucked, being barely more than plywood walls and a ceiling, but that didn't matter.

There had to be 30 Marines lifting or on the treadmills. One grunt was in full battle rattle, to include his gas mask, as he logged in the miles. I had to give him props, but that was something I didn't do.

As I looked around, I saw a Marine standing in front of one of the mirrors, arms pushed out as he checked his triceps, and immediately, my gaydar went off in full acquisition mode. It wasn't the mirror—all men flexed and posed in front of them. But as usual, I wasn't even aware of the how and why I could spot other gays from a mile away.

He was in his digi trou, t-shirt, and boots. Obviously fit with good definition, he wasn't bulky—more of a sprinter type. He was also flat-out gorgeous. And more pertinent, I would bet a million bucks that he was gay. He was a Marine, and we were in a combat zone, but still, I could look, and he was worth more than a few looks. And if I felt a little rush of lust, well, I'd been without getting laid for four months and counting, so could you blame me?

"Hey, dickwad, where you at?" B-man asked. "You're up."

I pulled my eyes away from the mystery Marine and laid down on the bench, heedless of my fellow corporal's sweat. I left the bar at 225, flattened my shoulder blades on the bench, and pushed out 12 reps with B-Man spotting. This was my fourth set, so that was about max for me, but at least I didn't need help to get the last rep up. My arms trembling, I stood, looking around for the Marine as I moved to spot Doc. He was gone. I wasn't sure how he'd managed that in the time in took me to finish my set, but he was definitely no longer in the gym.

I felt disappointed, which was pretty ridiculous. It wasn't like anything was ever going to happen. Like I said, I don't fuck Marines.

B-Man and Doc finished putting the four plates back on, and Doc laid out his Mickey Mouse towel. I turned my attention back to him as he got into position.

"Come on, Doc, ain't no thing there," I told him as he grunted to get the bar out of the cradle.

Chapter 3: Getting to Know Him

I was still riding high after I left the skipper's office. He wanted a full debrief, so I'd been in there with him and the first sergeant, going over everything I could remember. I'd been nervous as first, positive I was going to get my ass handed to me for not making sure the room had been cleared. To my surprise, neither had been too upset, and both had complimented me on my actions.

The muj we'd captured was some big-time bomb-maker, and he already had the ITT guys questioning him at the hospital. As soon as he was stabilized, he was on his way to Abu Ghraib, and then probably all the way back to Gitmo. The guy I'd killed was a foreign Al Qaeda handler, probably someone pretty high on the operational chain.

Just before I left, the skipper said I was being put in for an award, which was pretty freaking cool, even if I wasn't sure I deserved one. My dad and granddad would be proud, though. I wasn't going to tell them, however, until whatever was approved was going to be was pinned on my chest.

I'd just dumped my pack on my rack before going to see the skipper, and I still had Fallujah dust covering me. I also stunk to high heaven. But I was hungry, my stomach growling. One nice thing about being in the Sandbox was that some things didn't matter, and getting fed took precedence on getting cleaned up. I walked to the DFAC, ready to eat.

"Hey, Corporal Indigo," Chester said as he came out from the DFAC exit and spotted me. "Sorry about that back there. It was my bust. And thanks, you know, for saving my ass."

I was still pissed at him, but I was still pretty pumped as well.

"Look, you fucked up. OK, lesson learned. Don't let it happen again," I said, slapping him on the shoulder.

"I won't."

"OK, go get cleaned up. We're back out again tomorrow."

"Roger that."

I approached the clearing barrel at the entrance, stuck the muzzle of my M16 in, and pulled the trigger. Since I had the M203 attached, I opened it as a final check that I didn't have a grenade in it.

The welcomed smell of food wafted over me as I entered. Chow in the DFAC was damned good. I'd heard the government paid KBR $73 per day to feed each of us, so it had better be good. My stomach growled as the Filipino servers piled on pork chops, mac and cheese, and peas. I'd hit the salad bar, then eat what I had before coming back for a burger. Then it would be dessert time.

I entered the seating area, a large, low-ceiling building crammed with red-tableclothed tables and the same white plastic stacking chairs you could buy at Walmart. I automatically looked to the far right where the squad usually sat. They'd all left by now. I shrugged. I didn't need them to be able to eat, so any seat would do. I started to sit right there by the salad bar when I saw him.

My gym angel.

He was sitting alone, eating a salad.

Leave him alone, I told myself. *Don't get involved.*

Normally, I try to listen to myself. I knew I was attracted to him, but this was not the time nor place, and he was a Marine, too. Why even approach him?

But my body was still tripping on adrenaline, and the skipper's telling me I was going to get a medal filled me with braggadocio that overcame common sense. I walked right up to his table and sat down across from him.

"Is this seat free?" I asked, after-the-fact.

He looked up, and my heart caught in my throat. He said something along the lines that I'd already taken the seat, but most of that went right past me. I'm not much of a face guy. Give me a nice set of pecs, a six-pack, and a tight ass, and I'm in heaven. But this guy's eyes captured me, pulling me in. They were a weird sea green, a color I'd never really seen before on a guy, and I knew I could get lost in their depths.

I must have been gawking, because he asked "Are you OK?"

"Oh, sorry," I said, stammering a bit. "I just got back in from a patrol, and I'm a little wired up."

He took a sniff, but if he intended a slight, that was lost when he smiled and said, "Yeah, I can tell. About you coming in from patrol, I mean."

"I'm starving," I said, "and I didn't have time to clean up before eating."

No one really cared about that, so I knew I was just trying to fill the space between us with words, no matter how mindless.

"I'm Taylor Redding," he said, holding out a hand.

I took it, and an almost electric shock ran through my arm, which was more than disconcerting. That kind of thing didn't happen to me.

"And you're Corporal Indigo?" he added when I didn't say anything, making a point of looking at the name-patch sewn over my pocket.

"Ah, yeah. Alex Indigo. I'm with Bravo 1/1."

"I'm a 2799," he told me.

"What's that? You in comms?"

"Hell, no," he said, furrowing his brows, which almost made him look hotter. "Comms are twenty-five hundreds. I'm an ITT. You know, an Interpreter/Translator."

"No shit? You speak haji?"

This time, the slight clouding of his eyes sent off warning bells in my mind.

"I speak *Arabic*," he said, with emphasis on the word.

OK, "Arabic." He's one of those kind of guys.

"We just brought in an EPW," I said, making sure to use the official term for a prisoner. "They say he's a master bombmaker. Did you get in on that?"

"I heard about him, but no. That's for the counterintel guys, and I'm a little junior for that," he said, pointing to his own corporal insignia. "Sometimes we help them, but mostly, I go out with the commanders when they need to speak with the locals. A few times, I go on patrol with you grunts, especially on snatch missions."

"Like with captains? You interpret for them?"

"Captains, majors, all the way to the CG, if he needs us."

Fuck, he plays with the big boys, I thought. *I don't need to talk to anyone higher than the skipper if I can help it.*

"Um, I don't mean anything by this, but you don't look like a ha . . . like an Arab."

"I'm not. My family's Scottish, English, and a bunch more. I'm from New Braunfels, Texas."

"Texas? I'm from Altus. Altus, Oklahoma. That's just north of the Texas border. You know, enemy territory, 'Go Sooners' and all."

He smiled and said, "That's a long ways from me. Maybe a seven or eight-hour drive. And we're all A&M fans in the Hill Country."

"Oh, that sucks. An Aggie? Well, no telling for taste. At least tell me you're a Cowboy fan."

"Texans, not the 'Boys. And the Spurs, of course."

"Eh, I guess I can live with that. I don't have to find somewhere else to eat.

"So how did you learn Arabic. The Corps send you to that language school?"

"No, my dad was stationed there, and we were with him in the Saudi, Kuwait, and the UAE for almost nine years all told."

I was vaguely aware of where the UAE was, in the Middle East, at least, but I didn't want to profess my ignorance. This guy could speak Arabic, and it sounded like his English was better than mine. I didn't want him to think I was a dumb shit.

"I seen you, I mean, I saw you at the gym the other day," I said, mentally kicking myself for saying "seen" right after telling myself I didn't want to sound like a dumb shit.

"I'm a Marine, so yes, that's a logical place to find me," he said.

That could have sounded sarcastic, but with him, it seemed more of a joke.

"You know, got to keep the ladies interested," he added, making a which-way-to-the-beach pose, flexing his bicep.

Yeah, right. You don't fool me for a moment.

"Are you going to let your pork chops get cold?" he asked me. "I thought you told me you were starving."

And I realized I hadn't taken a bite yet.

"It's the scintillating conversation, doncha know," I said, cutting a piece of pork, but looking up at him to see how he took that.

He didn't acknowledge what I'd said, which was a bit of a letdown. It hadn't been much in the way of a flirt, but it had been only the opening salvo.

Hell, what am I thinking? I don't fuck Marines, I told myself for the hundredth time. *Get this guy out of my mind!*

The fact of the matter was, however, that I wanted to make an exception. It had been a long time, and something about Taylor had my nerves set on fire. It could have been what had happened today. Some guys said that killing a man was the biggest turn-on, that it hyped up the body. I don't know if that was true or not—in fact, it was kind of obscene, when you thought about it—but the bottom line was that I was horny as hell, and I wanted to bend him over the table right then and there.

Instead, I took a bite of pork chop. It was probably an urban myth, but people said that the cooks put saltpeter in our food to cut down on our libido. I thought that was bullshit, but if they had a big bucket of it back there, maybe I should just go back and guzzle a pound or two, because I was getting a rise. Marines almost all went commando, and if I stood up, well, my utility trou wouldn't hide much.

I started to talk, just to get my mind off of the images that had been forming in my mind. I was shocked when Taylor said he'd only been in for just under two years, and he was already a corporal. I guess the Corps needed ITT guys more than a simple grunt. It had taken me over three years to get my cutting score high enough for E4.

Too soon, though, he was finished eating. I tried to come up with something to say to keep him at the table, but it was drawing a blank.

"It was nice meeting you, Alex," he said as he stood up to police his tray. "I'll probably see you around."

"Yeah, I'll see you. Take it easy," I said, not standing up.

In fact, I had to sit there, more than a few minutes after he left before I could stand to get my desert. I don't know why I bothered, though. Anyone noticing would assume my hard-on was over the blueberry pie ala mode, and that was a good enough reason for anyone to get one.

Chapter 4: Living the Lie

Life at Camp Fallujah was a far cry from the battalion's last tour at Camp Falcon. This was veritable civilization. We had the Exchange, phone calls home, the DFAC, hot showers, the internet; all the comforts of home—if home was some barren outpost out in the middle of the desert. But compared to what it could be, no one was complaining. Hell, we even had gourmet coffee from Lindsey Coffee Company, out of Phoenix, who donated it all to us.

If we weren't out on a mission or taking care of some admin BS, we were usually catching some Z's, hitting the gym, or just playing some grab ass. Cards games were regularly in force, and guys who hadn't read a book since their high school English class had their nose buried in anything they could find. I-Pods were in hot demand to listen to tunes. But we also had a huge library of movies and television shows, all free to download. The quality sometimes sucked, but heck, I was surprised that the Corps allowed the movies on the computers.

Zim—Corporal Serge Zimmer—had brought a huge 17-inch HP laptop which became the "NCO Theater." We'd stick it on an empty wooden spool for some sort of cable that served us as a table and watch whatever he'd downloaded.

Today it was *X-Men*, which at six yerars old, was almost brand new for the library. As usual, we were all giving the movie a ration of shit. Wolverine was our primary target, and each of us figured we could take him out without too much of a problem. He might have the talons, but a SAW packed a bigger punch.

The other character of note was Mystique. Rebecca Romjin-Stamos might as well have been naked with only a layer of blue body paint between us and her skin.

With Mystique standing proudly in front of the camera, Zim grabbed his crotch and said, "I'd stick my gun in that clearing barrel."

"Clearing barrel" was a term sometimes used to describe the female Marines at the camp—but always out of their hearing. I hadn't heard it outside of that usage, but the meaning was clear.

“Fuck, you’re shooting blanks, Zim,” Ben said, tossing an empty Doritos wrapper at him.

“Don’t matter none if the wrigglers are gone; the jizz is still at max capacity.”

Zim had three kids already, and a corporal’s pay didn’t go far, so he’d had his tubes cut before we deployed.

“Look at her ass? I mean, it’s perfect! I’d make her scream with my big cock,” Zim said. “And no condom if she can’t get pregnant.”

“Fuck, Zim. A condom’s not just for that. It’s to stop disease,” I said.

Straight guys seemed to take too many chances with that, I’d noticed. Not like the gay community.

“I don’t wear a raincoat in the shower, Alex, so why use a rubber to fuck?”

“You don’t shower in toxic wastes, either.”

The other guys laughed, even Zim, but he said, “Does that ass look toxic to you? You telling me you wouldn’t hit that?”

Of course, the real answer was no. I wouldn’t “hit’ that. I’ve got nothing against women, and I can acknowledge that a woman can be beautiful, like a deer is beautiful. But I don’t fuck deer, either.

And of course, I said, “Damned straight I would, in a New York minute!”

“That’s all it would take you?” B-Man asked. “Mighty quick on the draw, there.”

“We’ve been here a long time, and the pressure’s building up. I’d probably blow right through her and out the top of her head.”

It had been a long time, and my thoughts momentarily flitted past the image of Taylor from when we ate together three nights ago. My words were about some Hollywood actress in a blue skinsuit, but my mind was on a certain ITT Marine.

“Don’t sleep with your mouth open tonight, B-Man. No telling what might get stuffed into it,” I said. “A man’s gotta get relief, doncha know.”

“Yeah, I always knew you were a fag,” B-Man said.

I wondered what B-Man would say if he knew I really was gay. And that was one of the things that bothered me about playing a part. I had to live a lie, joking about women, telling total bullshit stories about past conquests. I’d gotten to the point where I was telling real stories, just changing the names from Kevin to Kathy.

So it might seem odd that I’d tell B-Man to keep his mouth closed, but that was all part of my strategy. In Health Class one day at school, the lesson was on psychology, and the teacher had mentioned something called the Carrie Nation Syndrome. Carrie was an alcoholic who fought to push Prohibition through. The idea was that she outwardly fought against who she really was. It was like the evangelical television pastors who rail against the "evils of homosexuality," but then they're caught in bed with a 15-year-old chicken.

It seemed to me that lots of straight guys make the occasional gay comment. The whole teabagging thing was perpetuated by straight guys, after all. And since I'm playing the part of a very straight guy, confident about my sexuality, I wouldn't be above the "mouth open" joke sometimes, whether that was referring to teabagging or sticking my dick in it. You know, hiding in plain sight and all.

"On second thought, you're too fucking ugly, and that snaggle-tooth doesn't do you any favors," I said.

B-Man was actually embarrassed by the front tooth that stuck out and over at an angle, so that might have been hitting a little close to home. He gave me the finger and focused on Zim's laptop.

"Shit, I've had blue balls for a month now," Keenan Preston said.

"How can you tell?" Ben asked. "I mean, you know."

Keenan was black, so Ben was saying "blue" couldn't be seen. He leveled a wicked punch into Ben's thigh in response. The thud sounded painful, but Ben took it without even a grimace.

The talk gravitated back to Wolverine's talons, but my mind drifted. I was used to the machismo BS by now. I'd been doing it since I realized I was gay in junior high school. My dad had gone unaccompanied to Okinawa, so my mom took the three of us kids back to Altus, where we'd stayed even after he rotated back to the States for what we thought was his last tour before retiring. Then he got promoted to Master Guns, but Cicely was a junior, so we stayed in Altus so she wouldn't have to change for her senior year. And we stayed there, Dad joining Mom and Peter when he retired. I had already enlisted by then.

Altus is a small town, fewer than 20,000 souls, and being gay wasn't high on the acceptability meter, to say the least. So I knew to hide it. It might have been different if we'd joined Dad at Pendleton. As I discovered when I got my own orders there, just 35 miles away in San Diego, in Hillcrest, to be exact, was a thriving gay community. But if I'd come out in high school, I'd never have been able to enlist.

Bottom line was that I knew how to hide who I was. I knew how to live a lie. Someday, maybe, it wouldn't matter, but today, even with DADT, hiding who I am was a necessity.

Just a couple of years ago, a sailor named Jason Tiner was discharged from the Navy after appearing on the show "Boy Meets Boy." I guess by being on the show, he broke the "Don't Tell" part of the act, so he was just the latest Donald Duck.

It used to be worse, though, before DADT, so I should be grateful. They used to court martial gays and lesbians.

I don't fuck Marines now, but I did before—well, one Marine. I met Major Randall "Vulture" Fortinelli at the Brass Rail in Hillcrest one evening back in 2003. Vulture (he insisted I use his call sign) was a pilot at Yuma, and each weekend, he made the two-and-a-half hour trip to Hillcrest to cruise.

"Vulture" was an appropriate call sign. He was a chicken hawk and liked to hang out in Hillcrest, watching and waiting until he could pounce on some young guy, not necessarily a twink, but young. And I was young. Nineteen and a PFC, I was right in his gunsights. And me, naive dipwad that I was, I let the fact that he was a major overwhelm me. I met him half-a-dozen weekends while he regaled me with his worldliness until I caught him chatting up a kid who couldn't have been more than 15 and I dropped his ass.

But one of his stories was back pre-DADT, at Camp Lejeune when he was an aerial observer, an AO, for an infantry battalion. He was called to serve as a member of a court-martial of a chapstick lesbian out of the FSSG. Along with the other five members of the court, he listened as the prosecutor gave all the evidence that the lance corporal was, in fact, a lesbian. Then the defense lawyer called up a young cannon cocker out of 10th Marines. The PFC sat down and was sworn in, then the lawyer asked him if he ever had sex with anyone in the court. The PFC said yes and pointed at the lesbian.

The Vulture said that surprised him, because he was sure the lance corporal wasn't bi, but 100% lez. The lawyer asked him if he was sure, and the nervous PFC said yes, so the defense lawyer sat down with his proof that his client was straight. So, the prosecuting attorney got up, looking puzzled, and he asked the PFC if he had sex with her. The PFC said yes. He asked if he had intercourse with her. The PFC said yes. He started to turn away, then came back and asked the PFC to describe what happened.

The PFC was nervous, which I could understand. Here he was, sitting in front of the judge, who would have been a colonel, three officers and three SNCO's as members of the court, and he was asked about fucking a Marine. But he managed to get out that two

Saturday night's before, at the Area 10 E-Club, the defendant came up to him and asked him to dance. After two minutes on the dance floor, she asked him to follow her to the head, and then asked him to fuck her. He did, right there, not even getting undressed.

The lawyer asked to confirm the date, then pointed out to the members of the court that this was the week after the lance corporal was charged.

Then, the PFC, blurted out in a plaintive voice, "I told everyone what had just happened, but they all said bullshit, sir, and they said they didn't believe me!"

The Vulture told me, barely containing himself, that the lawyer said, "Don't worry, son, the court believes you."

The Vulture thought this was hilarious, and maybe it was funny in a way. I could picture the PFC trying to tell his buddies that he'd just gotten laid only to have no one believe him. But I thought the Vulture's uproarious laughter as he was telling several of us the story was almost traitorous. Here he was, a full, card-carrying fag, and he voted to convict the lance corporal and give her a Dishonorable Discharge.

I understood why he did that. His vote would not have been enough to acquit the lance corporal. And he was living the lie, just like I've been doing, just like that lance corporal did when she asked the PFC to fuck her. But, it just seemed dirty to me.

I've thought about that lance corporal often since then. I don't know her name or really anything about her, but I sometimes wonder what she's doing now and what she thinks of the Corps. And I admire her. If I had to fuck a girl to stay in the Corps, would I? Yeah, I would, if I could get it up, but I had my doubts about that. It sucks big time that it would ever come to that, but it is what it is.

Sometimes I wonder why I even bothered. If they don't want me, why don't I just leave? Why hide who you are? But I can't see doing anything else. As I looked at the six of us lounging around watching the Wolverine slash bad guys, it felt like home. These were my brothers, and I'd give my life for them—just as I knew they'd give their lives for me. White, black, Hispanic, Asian, straight, gay—none of that mattered when your blood coursed green.

Chapter 5: Family

"A Navy Commendation Medal with Combat 'V?' I'm proud of you, son, really proud," my dad said.

I didn't bother telling him that it was a Navy and Marine Corps Commendation Medal—he was old Corps, and I knew he would always use the old name for it.

"I want to tell Grandpa myself, so don't you spoil it, OK?"

"I won't. He'll be so proud."

Grandpa, Sergeant Major Marcus Indigo, had been awarded a Silver Star in Korea, earned at the Frozen Chosin. He'd been a grunt, just like me. The Navy Comm the first sergeant told me I'd be getting was nowhere near Grandpa's Silver Star, but I hadn't done anything near what he'd done when the Chinese had come streaming across the Yalu.

Dad had three Navy Comms and two Navy Achievements to go along with his retirement Meritorious Service Medal, but none of his Comms or Achievements had a Combat "V." Dad had been a Motor T Marine, driving 5-Tons and 7-Tons. He'd had one tour in Vietnam, but most of his career had been in peacetime billets, missing Grenada, Panama, and both Gulf Wars. He was as gung-ho as I was, but I'd already had two combat tours, and even if he'd been in Vietnam, he'd never heard a shot fired in anger. I think that was one of his big regrets in life.

I know it is stupid to want to run to the sound of gunfire. It makes no sense. But I also think that every Marine wants to prove to him or herself that they can measure up to all the Marines who've gone before them.

"Are you going to visit Grandpa when you get back?" Dad asked.

With Grandma gone, Grandpa had moved to Jacksonville, outside of Camp Lejeune. We knew he had all his retired Marine buddies there, but we all worried about him, and Dad, his sister, and his two surviving brothers tried to visit the sergeant major as often as they could. But despite all the grandkids, I was the only Marine in the third generation.

"Maybe we can go together. I'm even thinking about putting in for Lejeune when I re-enlist."

I knew Dad would prefer that I go to Lejeune. I'd come out to him before I enlisted, and he'd been very supportive of me, which was a godsend. But he knew of the draw of Hillcrest, and I think he'd rather have me at Lejeune without such a close and concentrated gay center of population. I'd told him I could keep things on the low-down, but I'm not so sure he was as confident of my discipline. To him, Lejeune was just a safer environment for me.

I chaffed a bit that he tried to control my career, but I knew I was damned lucky. I knew of two other gay Marines in the battalion. One told me that his family had disowned him when he came out, and he was essentially on his own. He'd received NJP for being UA by 12 hours and busted down a rank, so his chances of re-enlisting were pretty slim. He didn't know what he was going to do after his enlistment was up what with no family and no Corps. The other Marine, a sergeant, was afraid to tell his family. He'd even created a fake girlfriend, a lesbian in the Navy who wanted a similar cover for her family.

"I've been watching the news, son. Ramadi is getting pretty hot. No chance of you going there?"

All phone calls and internet were cut off when a Marine or soldier was killed until the next-of-kin were notified, and that had been happening quite often lately. That had become our bellwether on how things were going. It was bad in Sadr City in Baghdad, but it was worse in Ramadi.

I didn't think we would be sent there. Three-Eight was already in the city along with an Army brigade. But you never knew. My dad knew, though, that I couldn't pass any of that on the phone.

"Can't say, Dad. You know how it is."

"Yeah, yeah, I do. Sorry. I just worry about you."

"I know you do. I'm getting the high sign, though. My time's up, and people are waiting. Tell Mom I'm sorry I missed her, and tell everyone I love them."

"Roger that. I love, you, son, and keep your head down."

"Love you, too, Dad. Love you much."

I cut the connection and stood, the next Marine in line hurrying over to make his call. It was late at night, which was a good time to get a connection back to the States, but I did need to hit the rack. The platoon was going out to one of the outlying villages for a few days, and I wouldn't have an opportunity to call again until we were back, so the missed sleep was well worth it to be able to talk to my dad for a few moments.

Chapter 6: Flirting with Danger

Six days later, we were back at Camp Fallujah after sitting in the dust in a tiny collection of shacks out in the desert that served as a town. Technically, we were a TCP, or Traffic Control Point, watching for arms or muj's trying to slip back into Fallujah. In reality, we sat on our asses, with maybe ten or twelve vehicles a day passing through. Being outside of the wire tended to raise the pucker factor, but after a couple of hours, we'd been bored shitless. And with only MRE's and one haji mart where the Ali Baba running it charged us $5 for a warm Coke, we were happy to be back for decent food and hot showers.

I felt a little guilty that we weren't doing much. Like my dad had said, Ramadi was heating up, and Marines and soldiers were dying there. Even some SEALs had been killed. Still, we knew that could change in an instant. We'd had arty and air cover while out on the TCP, but if we'd been hit with any good-sized unit, it could have been hairy.

At the moment, though, my thoughts were just on getting some of the good DFAC food in my belly. MRE's are OK, and during cold weather training up at Bridgeport, they actually seemed pretty good. But out in the Sandbox, they left a lot to be desired.

I took my loaded tray out into the seating area, ready to join my squad, as normal, but a familiar profile caught my eye—familiar to my day dreams and one very convoluted real dream that I couldn't quite remember, but knew it had been graphically intense.

Taylor was sitting alone, as he'd been before, quietly eating his meatloaf and corn. I looked over to where the squad normally sat, and my squadmates were focused on shoveling real food down their throats as fast as they could. I only hesitated a moment—I'd just spent six days attached to them at the hip.

"I see you're eating with all your friends here. Mind if I join you, too?"

Taylor looked up, probably surprised that someone was speaking to him, then as he recognized me, a smile came over his face.

"Sure, I think we can find some room here," he said, waving an arm to take in the seven empty seats.

"Sorry about the dust again. Just got back from TCP duty."

He shrugged and said, "It's what we do. Well, it's what you grunts do, right?"

"It's not like you're a POG, Taylor. You said you go out with the grunts sometimes, so that makes you an honorary grunt."

"Oh, I'm honored," he said with a smile.

Some grunts took that POG-combat Marine seriously. But my dad had spent 30 years as a POG, so other than a little good-natured ribbing, I never did. Without POGs, the infantry couldn't fight.

Now a "fobbit" was another thing. My dad and probably grandpa called them REMFs, for "Rear Echelon Mother-Fuckers," but in the era of *Lord of the Rings*, we used "fobbit," and that was probably the worst thing you could call another Marine. I didn't joke around with that—but I would use it when it was deserved.

"So, you interrogate any ha . . . Iraqis lately?"

"Just the same old, same old. I did go with the CG to the police headquarters, though. It was all pretty boring, but you should have seen the spread they put out. The lamb was amazing," he said, pushing at the meatloaf with his fork in counterpoint. "Makes this taste like crap."

I took a bite of my own meatloaf, which had been buried on my plate under a scoop of gumbo. I wasn't sure what he was going on about. I liked lamb, but there was nothing wrong with this good KBR chow.

"They kept telling us that Al Anbar has the best lamb, Al Anbar had the best fish, Al Anbar had the best dates—"

"Wait, the best fish? We're in the middle of the desert," I said, pausing mid-forkful.

"The Euphrates is a pretty big river, Alex, and the Buhayrat al Qadisiyyah up at Haditha's a huge lake. Lots of fish."

"Oh, yeah, I guess so."

"You know, there's a story about a huge fish, or maybe a whale, that they called Al Anbar, that kept one of Mohammed's Armies alive. That's not where we get the name Al Anbar, though, which was Persian for 'warehouse.'"

"You know Muslim history?" I asked, surprised.

The smile faded from his face, and he looked down at his food, toying with his fork. Professing any interest is things Muslim was not a very popular thing to do in the Sandbox.

"Not that there's anything wrong with that. I'm just surprised. I have a hard-enough time with American history," I quickly added.

That seemed to mollify him, and he started into a rather long history lesson on the area that bounced back and forth between facts seemingly at random. I was impressed with his breadth of knowledge—not that I was actually taking in much of it, but more simply watching him as he lit up with the ability to share it with someone.

"Hell, you sure know a lot," I said when he had to stop to catch his breath. "You should be a professor."

"Well, I'm at UCI now."

"UCI?"

"University of California, Irvine."

"Oh, shit. Like to get a degree?"

"That's the normal reason to go, yes."

Fuck, I knew he was out of my league. A university boy?

I'd had a one-night stand with a San Diego State guy, but that was just animal sex. I doubt that we said more than 50 words together after we'd left the bar.

"So, I don't get it. If you're in school, how are you here?"

"I'm not a Cali citizen, so UCI's pretty expensive for me. So I joined the reserves to help out. But now the Corps needs me, so I'm taking off a year of school."

"You mean 'cause you speak Arab, right?"

"Arabic, yes. And I thought it was my duty."

"So, what are you going to do when you get back? I mean, after you graduate?"

He looked up as if to see if anyone was listening, then quietly said, "I want to go to OCS."

"You're going to be an officer?"

"That's the plan."

Fucking great. Now I'm sure he's out of my league.

Why I was concerned confused me. I was just talking to the guy, nothing more. Sure, I'd had a few fantasy moments with him as the subject, but as I've said a thousand times, I don't fuck Marines. And I certainly wasn't looking for a deep relationship out here in the Sandbox.

He had his head down again, but I could see him looking at me as if waiting for my response, and I realized he was apprehensive. For some unknown reason, many enlisted Marines felt embarrassed to admit that they wanted to become officers, and others derided them if they professed the desire. I thought that was bullshit. Why wouldn't a Marine want to become one? If I had the education, I might apply. There was nothing wrong with staying enlisted. We were the ones that actually won the battles, putting into play what the officers planned. But there was nothing wrong with being an officer, either.

"Hell, Taylor, that's great," I said, and I could see him relax. "And when you're Commandant some day, I can say I knew you when you were a lowly corporal like me."

"Shit, Alex," he said, but smiling.

He really has a gorgeous smile, I thought.

"You need a refill?" he asked, standing with his empty glass, as if he wanted to change the subject.

"Uh, sure. Bug juice, please," I said, taking a quick swallow to empty my glass.

Nice smile, nice ass, too, I thought as I watched him walk to the drink stand.

When he came back, our talk drifted to various subjects of no import. It was just nice to chat. Three other Marines sat down at the other end of the table, but I barely noticed them.

I did notice when B-Man came up behind me and said, "Alex, there you are."

I felt a rush of guilt, not that I should have, as I barely stammered out, "Oh, yeah. B-Man, this is Taylor. He's a corporal with ITT."

I had to force myself to cut off what could have become verbal diarrhea.

"Hi," B-Man said, then to me, "The gunny wants all NCOs at 1500."

"OK, thanks. I'll be there. So what about lifting?"

"He said it shouldn't take long, so 1600, OK?"

"Sounds good."

B-Man waited a few moments as if to see if I was going to leave with him, then said, "Well, uh, I'll see you then."

"B-Man's one of the other team leaders in my squad. He's a good guy."

"Why didn't you eat with him? I mean, him and the others. I see you eating there all the time with the rest of your squad."

Hell, he's noticed me? I wondered, feeling a small thrill.

"Fuck, I've just spent six days smelling all of their farts. We were on top of each other 24/7. I thought I'd join you seeing as you had an entire table to yourself," I said, trying to make light of it.

"Well, yes. I'm usually alone. No other E4's in ITT here."

Ah, that's why he eats alone. That must suck.

I knew that even surrounded by thousands of Marines, he was probably lonely. And I wanted to help make it better for him.

Before I could second-guess if it was a good idea or not, I said, "And that's why you lift alone in the gym. Not smart. So tell you what. Are you free at 1600 today?"

"Yes, I can be. Why?"

"Why? So you can lift with us. You need a spotter, and we can always use a fresh perspective on things."

"I don't know . . ."

"Of course you do. They're good guys, all of them. You'll like them."

"I don't want to intrude. I know how tight you guys get."

He was objecting, but I could tell he wanted to accept. It was written all over his face that he needed companionship.

And that was all it was for me. Nothing deep. Just helping out a fellow Marine, like I would any Marine.

I was pretty sure of that, at least.

He still hesitated, so I said, "You really need a spotter when you lift. It's regs. Your team's mission would suffer if you dropped a stack on your neck and weren't there to do your translating, right?"

"Well, right."

"So, 1600. No arguments. Just be there."

He hesitated a moment, and on pins and needles, I acted as nonchalantly as possible, scraping up the past of my gumbo and putting it in my mouth.

"Yes, you're right. Why not? I'll be there at 1600."

There was really no reason to feel the huge rush of relief that swept over me. No reason at all. And there was no reason to feel so happy when he picked up and policed his tray.

So why did I want to break out in song?

Chapter 7: Lifting with the Guys

So why hell am I so fucking nervous? Calm the fuck down, Alex!

We were already at the gym, staking out one of the benches. Our mission tempo made it so we couldn't keep a regular work-out schedule, but Doc Possum decided we were doing chest and arms today, and it was easier just to accept and leave it at that.

Taylor hadn't shown up, and it was 1608. I wondered if he'd canceled, and that made me surprisingly sad.

Shit, I'm like a high school girl. What the fuck?

This was probably a bad idea in the first place. Worst case was that the guys would come off as cretins—which was not out of the realm of possibility, knowing them. Or maybe the worst case was that Taylor would come across as a like a queen, effectively outing me. That one wasn't as likely, but with him still not arriving, my mind was grasping at all possible outcomes.

I didn't like the way I was feeling. I've never been a worry wart. And I'd never fallen for someone, not the Vulture, not Hank Gibbons, my first fuck, and this certainly wasn't the time nor place for it. I needed to get my head on straight, or I could be a liability outside the wire where bad shit really could happen.

"Oh, hey, Taylor!" I shouted with relief upon seeing him walk in, forgetting what I'd just been telling myself.

"Guys, that's Taylor Redding. B-Man, you met him today. He needs a spotter, so I told him he could work out with us. No NCO's in his unit."

"No NCO's? What unit?" Doc asked.

"ITT. You know, interrogators."

"Did he interrogate Saddam?" B-Man asked.

"Uh, I don't think so," I said as Taylor hesitantly came up.

"Did you interrogate Saddam?" B-Man asked him.

"What? Uh, no. That was three years ago, and I came here with you, with I MEF. Besides, he was held at Camp Cropper, and only the Army and CIA had their hands on him, not Marines."

B-Man shrugged, then asked, "So have you water-boarded anyone yet? What's that like?"

"Shit, B-Man, what, you're the interrogator now? Give the guy a break. He's just here to break a sweat," I told him.

"Good to meet you. I'm Crispin," Doc said, as always giving his real name, not that it ever did any good.

"He's Doc Possum, our corpsman," Lance Corporal—and ex-corporal—Lyle Fleisher said. "And I'm Lyle, that's B-Man, and you're Taylor. So now that the bullshit is finished, let's get back to lifting."

We were lifting 135 for the first set to warm up, and I could see the slight relief in Taylor's eyes. With Doc there, he probably thought we were going for the heavy stacks. All of us were pretty cut, I had to admit. But Doc was huge, almost to body-builder size, which was rare in the Corps. We didn't lift for huge muscles, but rather to be able to do our jobs, and our missions didn't allow us to follow what true body-builders had to do each day even if we wanted that. Doc just had the genes for getting big, I guess.

Lyle had just completed his warm-up set, the last of us to push it out, so he got off the bench, with one hand indicating it was Taylor's turn.

"Do you need to stretch out first?" I asked him.

"No, I can stretch with that," he said, laying on the bench.

I moved in back of him to spot, standing easy. One-thirty-five was nothing, but it was good form to have someone there in case the lifter slipped. He lifted the bar and proceeded to push out ten reps, all slow and steady, all with good form. Looking down on him, I couldn't help but to watch his pecs as the flattened and bunched with each rep. Except for Doc, none of us were huge, but we all had some bulk. Lyle was the smallest of us at 180 lbs (we all knew each of our weights for when we had lifting-your-own-weight competitions), but I doubted Taylor tipped the scales at 150. As I had noticed before, he had more of a runner's build. Still, with almost none of that 150 being fat, his chest looked pretty good as he completed his set.

I felt the tiniest twinge in my crotch as I watched, the briefest image of him lying on his back in another, more intimate setting, before I banished the thought, replacing it with an image of a photograph I'd seen in a history book of a WWII Nazi atrocity where they'd hung a passing businessman.

I know that's pretty fucked up, but that was my go-to mental image to quash my libido, and it always worked. I'm not sure why that image, and I'm not going to sit down with a shrink to figure it out.

With the warm-up set out of the way, we loaded two more 45 lb plates on the bar. Taylor's eyes widened ever-so-slightly, so I moved closer and quietly asked, "Is that OK?"

"Should be," he said, but not sounding overly confident.

"We can knock it back when you're up. It's no big deal. We do it all them time depending on who's with us."

"No, no. It's OK. No problem."

"To failure, right?" Doc asked as he put his Mickey Mouse towel on the bench.

I caught Taylor's smile as he saw the towel.

"Fucking A right, to failure," B-Man said. "I'm hitting a new high today."

When we lift to failure, that is, keep lifting until we fail on the last attempt, spotting was even more important. Lyle took his position behind him, and then Doc started.

"One, two, three . . ." we started, as we counted out his reps.

Doc was big, and Doc could lift more than any of us as a 1RM, or "one rep maximum," but he didn't have the stamina reflective of that. He started wobbling at 20, then with us shouting him on, managed to get another two before Lyle had to help him seat the bar back in the cradle.

B-Man was next, hitting 26 before failing, then Lyle jumped in front of me and managed to put up 21. Then it was my turn. Back at Pendleton and between deployments, I'd hit 32 before, but here in the Sandbox, my best was 25. The daily grind of being a combat Marine broke us down. I lay back, flattening out my shoulder blades, and with a grunt, cleared the bar from the cradle, waited a moment, and began.

My style, which was wrong, according to all the experts, was to hold my breath for the first five reps, then get into a normal breathing pattern. The bar seemed particularly heavy, and I didn't think I'd reach even 20, but I kept pushing out the reps. At 15, my arms started to burn, but I kept going, my mind focused on just getting the bar up. I put everything into it, willing the bar to rise, blocking out my friends.

Until a single "Come, on, Alex! Five more!" broke through to my consciousness.

It was Taylor.

I was at 22, and ready to stop, but suddenly, I had to get those five more. I brought the bar down to my chest, and with a sudden surge of power, I forced it up. Down again, up again. That was two. I hesitated a moment, arms trembling.

"Don't wait. Hit it!" Lyle shouted into my face from where he was spotting me.

Down. Up. That was three.

There was no way I could get two more, I knew. But maybe one more?

Down, almost bouncing it off my chest as I lifted my ass off the bench to will the bar up one more time. Lyle moved in to help, but I shouted "I've got it," and finished the lift by myself.

"One more!" Taylor shouted, excitement in his voice.

I was done, my arms shot, but something drove me forward. I'd never do this while lifting alone, but I trusted Lyle, so before I even realized it, the bar was back down, and with every ounce of energy left in my body, I shot the bar up, pushing it back at the same time to try and catch the cradle hooks. Whether I would have made it in without Lyle or not, I didn't know, but he kept saying, "That was all you," so I was going to take it as a win.

"Good fucking job," Doc said, hand out to high-five me as I sat up.

I fist bumped Lyle, B-Man, and Taylor, feeling pretty damned good about myself. We still had three more sets before we started pyramiding up, and I'd probably shot my wad for those, but 27 here in Iraq was sweet.

And for Taylor to see me do it was sweeter.

And I knew that was messed up. I lifted with my squadmates. They were my brothers, and this was a team effort, in a way. I barely knew Taylor. But the fact was that I wanted to impress him.

I stood up and moved around behind to spot Taylor. I'd always thought it would be smarter to spot before lifting, but this was Doc's way, and we just went along with it. I shook out my arms, then stood in back of the bench as Taylor got into position.

"Just tell me, and I'll help lift it off."

He nodded, placed his hands on the bar, took them off, and placed them one more time, playing with the grip. He took five deep breaths, then nodded and said, "OK."

I lifted up, my tris barking out their complaints, and helped him center the bar over his chest before letting go. I could tell that Taylor was having trouble with the weight. He really should have scaled down 20 or 40 pounds. No one would have blinked at that, but I understood where he was coming from. The first time lifting with a group, and he wouldn't want to be labeled as a wimp, even if we wouldn't. When B-Man first joined the battalion, he could barely lift 225 once, and now he was pushing out 26 reps. Sergeant Jackson was more in the 155 lb-range on the bench, and no one thought less of him. Of course, with him, he could run any of us into the dirt and leave us puking on ourselves, so there was that. The point was that it wasn't the weight that mattered but the effort.

Taylor brought the bar down slowly, keeping nice form but tiring out his arms. His first rep was smooth, his second not quite as smooth, and his third was wavering with his left arm lagging the first, tilting the bar. I reached out to help the left side up, but he pushed forward, getting both arms locked.

He was breathing hard, his face red, and he lowered the bar again. This time, there was no way he was going to make it, so I helped him up as he let out a shout.

"That was mostly you," I said as I started to help guide the bar back to the cradle.

"One more!" he said.

Doc was standing at the foot of the bench, and he lifted his eyebrows and gave a grudging-looking nod.

"OK, let's do it," I said.

He brought the bar down quicker, hitting his chest and bouncing it up a couple of inches before gravity started winning the battle. I pushed my hands forward to help, and he yelled out, "I've got it!"

No, he didn't. But I tried to minimally assist him, letting him take as much of the weight as possible. He started writhing on the bench in the way casual lifters did when they tried to lift too heavy, and his face screwed up as if he was having an orgasm.

Mother fuck! Not an orgasm, idiot! I thought, trying to banish the image of Taylor, lying under me, writhing and with his orgasm face. *Just relax.*

I brought back the Nazi image, and it worked. I was back to normal. But with Taylor's hot exhalation hitting my crotch, my traitorous dick still stirred, not enough for anyone to notice, but enough to let me know it was interested.

Taylor finished his rep—with a big assist from me, and we got the bar back into the cradle. He sat up, swinging his arms back and forth to get rid of the lactic acid buildup.

"I haven't lifted for a while," he said, looking up at the other guys.

"You're doing it now, and that's what counts," Doc told him.

For the biggest and strongest among us, Doc was the one who always gave the most encouragement, unlike B-Man who could be a little demeaning at times.

I patted Taylor on the shoulder, and he got up, still looking a little sheepish. Normally, he'd have been the one to spot Doc, but I didn't know if he knew how, and judging from his form on the bench, probably not. So, I kept my position as Doc put on more plates for his lift.

Taylor might be gorgeous, but he obviously wasn't a gym rat. The fact that he showed up and did his set, however, was admirable in its own right. Not many guys had a strong enough self-image to be shown up by other guys in anything like this.

We each did another set. I probably over-lifted again. I was showing off, I knew, and that was pretty immature. It didn't stop me, though.

As Taylor got on the bench again, Doc adjusted his form. He knew knew his stuff—Taylor managed to get up three more reps.

On my next set, to my utter horror, I let out a wet-sounding fart on my fifth rep. The guys burst out laughing and making dramatic gestures as to the smell, even Taylor. I'd been concentrating so hard on my lift that I couldn't even tell if it had been a clean fart or a shart.

I got the bar back in the cradle and muttered, "Fucking DFAC chow," as if accusing them.

I knew I had to check my shorts, which were mercifully black, so if I had sharted, it wouldn't be that obvious.

"I've got to use the head," I said.

"Clean the bench first!" Taylor said. "I'm not putting my back on that."

B-Man threw a towel at me, then tossed the spray bottle. I felt my face redden and I wiped down the bench. I hooked the spray bottle on the edge the bin, threw in the towel, and headed off as Doc moved in to spot Taylor. A few catcalls followed me out of the gym.

I crossed to the head, entered one of the empty stalls, pulled down my shorts, and checked them. They were dry, thank goodness. I leaned back with relief, embarrassed, but it could have been worse. I'd wanted to impress Taylor, not make a fool of myself.

I thought of spotting him, of feeling his breath on my crotch, and my dick stirred. It had a mind of its own and didn't care if I'm almost shit myself. And that got me imagining things, things that shifted and morphed into Taylor on some king bed in a tropical cabana, palm trees swaying outside in the breeze. And, of course, that made my dick even harder.

I prided myself for always being on control of myself. I planned things out, and I never let the spur of the moment decide what I was going to do.

But in this case, I thought, *Fuck it.*

I reached down with my right hand and started stroking. That might seem rather crass, jacking-off in a communal head, gym shorts down around my ankles while I sat on a shitter. It actually wasn't that odd. Lots of guys did it. I was more of a sock-on-the-dick-at-night-in-the-rack kind of guy, but young men, a long time apart from lovers, will do what they have to to relieve the pressure.

I'd actually jacked-off the night before, so it should have taken a while, but the image of Taylor, naked, orgasming Taylor, was too much for me. Fifteen or twenty seconds later, I exploded, my mind lost in a universe of light and heat, and too quick for me to have toilet paper ready. I spluged across the stall and hit the back of the door. The jizz hung up for a moment before it started its slow descent down the white door. I grabbed some toilet paper, wiped it up, then looked for any missing globs.

My cock was still pulsing as it slowly relaxed. I wiped the head, then waited until it was limp enough, its mission completed, to be stuffed back under my shorts. My mind was a whirl of confused emotions. On the one hand, that was my best, most intense orgasm in years, so I should be happy. On the other hand, I'd just let something control me, something I hadn't wanted. Getting a hard-on during a lifting session? What the hell was wrong with me? I liked to be in control at all times, and this was the polar opposite.

It might be better if I just dropped all contact with Taylor, if not for my sanity, then to keep my place in the Corps. I did not want to do something stupid and get kicked out.

"Hey, man, you free in there. We've got people waiting!" a voice shouted out while the guy pounded on the door.

"Yeah, just a second."

I made an effort to be as noisy as possible as I pulled some paper off the roll. I even wiped my ass, which was probably taking it too far. I stood up, and almost opened the door when I realized I hadn't flushed.

I heard the blatt of someone in the next stall having a rough go of it, and as I opened the door, another Marine almost pushed me out of the way. Three other Marines were in line, all looking in distress. Behind me, the Marine who'd taken my stall must have barely had time to pull down his trou when he exploded.

"Fucking chow here," I said, to the nods of the waiting Marines.

I walked outside into the blazing heat, then back to the gym where Taylor was on the bench again, this time with 205 on the bar.

With Lyle spotting, he got in eight reps that I saw. I put a painful-looking expression on my face as I walked up.

"Everything come out OK in the end?" B-Man asked.

"Yeah, fucking comedian, B-Man," I said with a scowl.

"You've got one more set before we start pyramiding. Think you can get them in without stinking up the place?" Lyle asked.

"Yeah, I think I can manage."

I got down on the bench, as as I did so, I felt a tiny bit of cum leak out, a small post-ejaculate gift from my ever-generous cock. If they even bothered to notice, I hoped they'd think it was just piss. I didn't get in as many reps as the first time, but I didn't fart again, either, so I took that as a victory.

Taylor was fitting in with the guys as we moved to pyramiding, and I was pleased with that. But as I watched him, I knew I needed to drop any interest in him. I was attracted to him, but I couldn't afford to get involved with not only a fellow Marines, but one there with me in a combat zone. If I got involved with him, it would be too difficult to hide, and my career could be over.

And that's even assuming the guy likes me, I thought.

No, it was better not to go down that path. The risk was just too great.

Chapter 8: Dreamland

The next day, the platoon was out of the wire again, this time guarding an overpass on the route that the Dreamland water Marine and his seven Sudanese truckers used every day to bring water to the ISF. "Dreamland" was Camp Baharia, one of Uday's resorts, then an Army base, FOB Volturno, and then back to Camp Bahria after the Marines took over before the Second Battle of Fallujah.

Every day, some Marine from the FSSG, I guess, took his haji drivers and picked up filtered water from the lake on the base and delivered it to the Iraqi soldiers at their base. It was a sucky mission. This wasn't 2004 anymore, so it wasn't suicide to be out in a convoy, but the muj would love nothing better than to stick it to the ISF, who they considered traitors, and taking out their water supply would do the trick.

Hell, half of the ISF were muj in disguise. That was probably an exaggeration; the ISF was pretty useless, and if more were actual muj, they could probably put up a better fight. But the blue-on-green killings of American and Brits were done by the ISF soldiers on our side. I've been lucky never to have to work with them, and to put my ass on the line to bring them water would suck.

But some cooperative had probably said there was a hit being planned, so here we were, camped out in the sand. No air conditioning, no hot chow, nothing. We weren't even in a real FOB with walls and overhead cover or HESCO barriers. We had netting over our head which didn't cut out the sun's rays, and we had a cathole behind us, an MRE box turned on its side over it to act as a toilet. This was the norm just a year or two ago, but civilization had spoiled us. How did they expect us to survive without internet or pogey bait?

One of the boots in Third Squad actually said something to that effect, and he sounded serious. If his own squad hadn't given him a beat-down, I'm sure some of the rest of us would have.

It was probably good for me, though. Yesterday, at evening chow, I'd come into the DFAC, gotten my food, and turned, as usual, to go to our table. To my surprise, Taylor was there with the guys. I stopped dead, then put my tray on a half-full table and acted like I was getting a drink. Only I just abandoned it and left it there. We normally ate in DFAC 2, so I hiked over to DFAC 1 to get fed. I wasn't that hungry anymore, but I knew we'd be gone for the next who-knows-how-long, so I had to eat. I beat the guys back to the squadbay, and when they came in, I told them my stomach was acting up. By now being out here in the middle of nowhere, I could put Taylor out of my mind.

Well, I could try, at least. It helped that I didn't have to see him.

Several times, we could hear firefights break out in the city, but things remained quiet around us. The water Marine and his drivers passed by without incident. I'll have to say this, for a POG, that Marine had a set of balls on him.

On the third day, the lieutenant was getting as antsy as the rest of us, but he had the power to do something about it. He told the skipper that he was going to talk to the water Marine, and taking Ben and my teams for security, we loaded up two hummers for the quick trip to Dreamland.

The camp, home to a reserve unit, 1/25, was more austere than MEK, the official name for what we called Camp Fallujah. But it was a hell of a lot better than our CP at the overpass. And get, this—the lake where they got their water? Marines were fucking fishing there, with real fishing poles and all, like they were back in the States. We couldn't believe it. Like all US facilities, Dreamland got its share of mortars and rockets, but these guys were casting rods, using beef jerky as bait, of all things, and pulling in catfish as big as my arm.

This was one crazy-ass war. In Ramadi, just down the road, guys were getting killed every day. Here, reservists were fishing.

I'd worked with the reservists a couple of times. They might be based out of Dreamland, but they still patrolled in the city and outlying areas. And despite what we active duty Marines might sometimes say about reservists, these boys were good. They'd lost more than a few Marines in the fighting, too, so they weren't fobbits.

The lieutenant made it official and "conferred" with the water Marine for all of five minutes, and then we took care of the real purpose of the visit. After three days, almost all of us were out of our pogey bait, so Ben and I took our teams to the Dreamland's haji mart and about filled our packs with whatever we could, paying with the money the rest of the platoon had gathered. It looked like we had quite a haul, but with 38 Marines and three corpsmen, it wouldn't go that far.

We scored some hot chow before leaving. The mess-hands even gave us food to go when we told them about the rest of the platoon.

As we were loading back up on the hummers, laden down with chow and pogey bait, two mortars hit about 100 meters away. That didn't seem to bother the five Marines down around the lake who didn't let that interrupt their casting.

I don't know if the "Dreamland" was from Uday Hussein's time, or if that was after we got here, but the name fit. If I hadn't seen this place with my own two eyes, I would have thought it was something dreamed up by some Hollywood writers who'd never seen a war zone.

Chapter 9: What a Fucked-up World

I wished I smoked, I thought, as I sat in the darkness on the concrete table by the closed haji mart.

I was pretty conflicted, and smoking, for once, sounded better than just sitting there stewing in my thoughts. Sometimes, maybe most times, I just didn't understand the world.

I hadn't seen Taylor for almost two weeks, which had been a relief. Our schedules just didn't match. But cutting across camp this evening, I bumped into him as he got out of the front seat of a gun-hummer, a full bird colonel getting out of the back. He was in his flak and helmet, and he had his M4, but without full battle-rattle and looking pretty clean. The colonel thanked and dismissed him as I hung back, curious despite my promise to myself to keep clear of him.

"Hey, Taylor," I said, walking up as he turned towards his barracks.

"Oh, hi, Alex," he said, but seeming to be somewhere else.

"You just get back from somewhere?"

"Oh, yeah, the Green Zone."

"The Green Zone?"

I'd never been to the Green Zone, the highly-secured area around the US embassy in Baghdad. I'd heard stories about "chu-ville," where everyone had two-man rooms in a CHU (which was like an air-conditioned shipping container), swimming pools, a big PX, even a Subway. I'd kill to make a trip there just to see what it's like.

"Yes. I was with the colonel for an embassy function."

"So, you just hang out with colonels?"

"You know how it is. I was supposed to be his aide, but he really wanted me to circulate and listen to what people were saying."

"Like a spy?"

Taylor smiled at that, a smile that quickly faded as he said, "Yes, something like that. He didn't want a local terp, and I guess he thought people would say things when I was around."

"So. . . ?"

"So, what?"

"So, did you hear anything?" I asked eager to know.

"Yes. No. I mean yes, I heard things. Not much in Arabic, though."

I knew he was bothered by something, so I asked, "What about in English?"

He took a deep breath, as if considering what to say, then obviously coming to a conclusion, he said, "Well, yes, there was one freaking story I heard."

"And . . . ?"

"I guess it isn't classified or anything, and it just shows how messed up these guys are."

I wasn't sure who "these guys" were, but I just let him talk.

"You know, in Baghdad, most of the fighting is red on red."

He meant Iraqi on Iraqi.

"The Sunni hate the Shia, and the Shia hate the Sunni. Sometimes they kill their own people just to foment more hate and incite more violence.

"Well, because of that, many Iraqis carry two ID cards, one with a Sunni name, one with a Shia name on it. That way, they can show the right one to whoever is manning the roadblock or coming into their home."

I'd heard something like that, and it was pretty fucked up. I looked at all ragheads as the enemy—it was safer to do that. But I knew that most of the rag—uh, most of the people just wanted the fighting to stop. I couldn't imagine being back in Altus and having to guess what church card, Methodist or Baptist, I'd have to pull out not to get myself killed.

"Anyway, while I was wandering around, this fag was talking to some people."

You're slipping, Taylor, I thought.

He'd said "fag," but without any of the disdain that a straight guy who didn't like gays would use. Normal guys who didn't care who we slept with wouldn't use "fag." Only the haters used the term—and us gays, much like blacks use "nigger" among themselves. It was one of those we-can-use-the-word-but-you-can't things.

"He said he was on a bus the week before when it was stopped by some gunmen. They came in and demanded that the passengers show their IDs. He pulled out his Sunni one, thinking the gunmen were Sunni, but it turned out he was wrong."

Woah! Sucks to be him. But he evidently survived.

"So he gets pulled out of the bus with 12 other men, and they're told to kneel in the sand. He said he knew he was going to die, so he started praying when the Shia shot the first man in the head.

Holy shit!

"They start going down the line, shooting each one in the head, execution-style. Just before the gunman stepped up to each guy, someone else pulled down their shirts behind them, making them sort of handcuffs."

"Handcuffs?" I asked interrupting.

"That's what he said. I guess when you pull them down, they keep someone's hands behind him," he said, pulling his arms back as if demonstrating.

"OK, if you say so."

"Not me, him. But anyway, when they pulled down his shirt, they saw he had a shaved chest."

"So?"

"Evidently, gay men shave their chests in Iraq. It's their thing."

I filed that nugget away. Not that I would make use of that intel. Getting caught with another guy might get me discharged, but getting caught with an Iraqi would put me in the brig. Not just a guy, but an Iraqi woman, too. Fraternization with the locals was a big no-no.

"So when they see this, they went bat-shit crazy on him, screaming that he was Satan himself, that he was damned to hell, that being gay was against the Koran."

I simply couldn't imagine being in that position. What could you do?

"So, do you know what they did to punish him for being gay?"

I shook my head.

"They beat him, then they raped him."

What the fuck?

"You said they raped him?"

"That's what he said. They pulled off his pants and three of them raped him in his ass, all the time screaming that he was damned to hell."

"That makes no fucking sense!"

Taylor shrugged and said, "No, it doesn't. And get this. After they raped him, they just left him there in the sand while they killed the rest. It was as if they thought that being raped like that was worse than death."

I was stunned. I'd never heard of such fucked-up logic in my life.

"Was he, I mean, did you think he was telling the truth?"

"I don't know. I'm just an interpreter, not an interrogator, so I don't have training in all the tells. But yes, I think he was. The other NGO and diplomat-types thought he was. They said this was proof that the Iraqi government had to act on gay rights."

"Man, that is totally fucked up. Did you tell the colonel?"

"Yes, on the ride back."

"What did he say?"

"He said we can't condone that kind of action, but maybe it was good riddance."

I felt a rush of anger flow through me. How dare that asshole say something like that. Fragging an officer is more of an urban legend than anything else, but for the moment, I was tempted.

"What do you think?" I asked, waiting to hear if Taylor would come clean to me about being gay.

"I'm not paid to think. I just listen and translate."

If you become an officer, someday you'll have to think, and you won't be able to hide behind your corporal's chevrons.

"I swear," I said, "I'll never understand these people. If we have to fight the Russians or the Chinese someday, fine. I'll fight them. But I think I can understand them. These Arabs, though, I just don't get their logic."

"There's a lot about their culture that is admirable, Alex."

"What, like killing guys just because they're riding a bus, and then raping a guy because he's gay? How the hell can they get a fucking hard-on to rape him. I couldn't get hard to fuck a . . . guy," I said, almost slipping in my anger and saying "woman."

"No, of course not. Just don't damn them all. Our culture isn't perfect, either."

I didn't want to listen to any more. I love my country, and despite all the shit here in the Sandbox, or maybe because of it, I was certain of our cultural superiority. We may have some bad shit at home, but nothing like what he'd just told me.

"Oh, so the college boy is some raghead lover," I said, with emphasis on the word "raghead."

He pulled back in surprise at my words and tone.

"I'm not surprised. Well, you can hang out with them all you want. I'm outta here," I said before stalking off.

"Alex . . ." I heard him call out, but I kept walking.

I'd been about to out him, too, telling him I knew he was gay, but I held back. I wasn't going to turn on one of my own kind.

I wandered around for awhile, my mind churning with a mash-up of thoughts. I found myself sitting on the concrete table by the haji mart as darkness enveloped the camp.

I sometimes felt sorry for myself, first for living in a town where I couldn't let people know who I really was, then joining the

Corps that I loved so much, but from which I had to live my lie. I hated the Westboro Baptist Church, the "God Hates Fags" church, both for their beliefs and for protesting at funerals for fallen Marines, soldiers, sailors, and airmen. I felt righteous anger and a desire for revenge when I heard about young men and women being beaten or even killed for being gay.

But that paled in comparison to what was happening here, not just in Iraq, but throughout the Middle East. Simply being gay was the death penalty in most of these countries. And here in Iraq, it was evidently considered worse than death to be raped, then left crying in the dust.

Given the choice, I'd rather be raped than killed. The guy was alive to tell his story. But the idea that he'd been punished more by being raped by angry men was extremely disconcerting. I just felt disconnected to humanity at the moment.

And then there was how I stormed off from Taylor. I was pissed that he'd tried to defend these people, but I knew I was more pissed at our position in the world at large, and I'd taken it out on him. I wanted to track him down and apologize, but it was probably better like this. I'd wanted to cut back on our contact, and now, I'd pretty much cut him off. It wasn't the way I'd have wanted it, but it was what it was.

I knew I should get back to the guys. They'd probably be playing cards, and I could get lost in that. No one promised me that this life would be easy, either as a gay man in the Marines, or simply as a Marine in Iraq. There is a saying that we have when things are shitty that helps us cope, and now seemed like a pretty good time to remind myself of it. I stood up, and before turning back to the squadbay, I said it aloud.

"Embrace the suck."

Chapter 9: Go Broncos!

"No, no! I'm not going!" I shouted as the tall blonde in her little blue skirt and tiny orange and white top pulled on my arm.

It didn't help that B-Man, Doc, and Ben were pushing me out of my chair—not that I was putting up a fight. But there were appearances to uphold, and no grunt was going to rush the stage to dance.

I sure wanted to, though. I'm not one of your theater-loving, artsy-fartsy gay guys. One of my favorite hook-ups in Hillcrest was, and he always had me in stitches, but I wouldn't know a timpani from a pirouette. But these were the Denver Broncos cheerleaders, and that was my team.

We didn't have a team in Oklahoma, so we went looking for "our" team. My dad was a diehard Cowboy fan, my mother a Chiefs fan, but my sister and I were Broncos fans. It had only been seven years ago that John Elway had led the Broncos to two Super Bowl wins, and Cecily and I had been beside ourselves with excitement. And now, the USO had brought the cheerleaders here to Camp Fallujah where they were in the middle of a show.

I was surprised how well-behaved my fellow-Marines were. Of course, we had the CG in the audience, but for a couple thousand sex-starved Marines, they hooted and hollered, but most of the shouts were within the bounds of civilized behavior, even considering all the "I love you's" that were shouted out.

The 12 cheerleaders weren't just crying out "Go Broncos!" They had dance routines, they had some guests—most of who I didn't know from Adam—and they brought up a lot of Marines and sailors for audience participation. It seemed as if almost all the WM's in the audience made it up to the stage and some point or the other, and more than a few of the male Marines, too. The gunny had already been up on the stage, but when asked to dance, he barely moved, much to our delight. Another gunny from the I MEF-Forward staff, though, danced his freaking ass off, also to our delight. Even the cheerleaders had to stop and watch, applauding him when he was finished, and with two of them flanking him with a simultaneous kiss.

I'd been praying that one of them would select me. I was at the end of an inside row of chairs, but each time they came out trolling the mass of Marines and sailors, they passed me by—until the tall blonde grabbed my hand. Still loudly protesting, I let the 110-pound girl drag me down the aisle and up on the stage where another ten or so Marines were waiting.

"OK, now that all you big, bad Marines—"

"And sailors!" one of us, a corpsman shouted, pointing to his crow.

"OK, Marines and sailors!" the head of the program said as every sailor in the place cheered. "As you know, being a cheerleader is hard work. It takes a lot of time and effort to keep our bodies fit."

She waited for the obligatory catcalls and cheers.

"But we know Marines—and sailors—are fit, too, so we want to take you through a routine with us. Can you hang?" she asked, the challenge implicit in her tone and body language.

More cheers from the crowd.

"So, please follow along with Kelsey and Keela . . . if you can!"

A couple of us whipped off our blouses, and we stood there, in utes and boots, ready for whatever they could throw at us.

The first thing the two cheerleaders did was to step forward, flinging their arms up and turning. I'm sure there was a formal name for the move, but I'm just a dumb grunt, and I followed along the best I could. Then there was the series of jumps, twists, spins, and more things than I could think of. At one point, I either zigged when I should have zagged, or the staff sergeant next to me fucked up, because we both collided hard. He fell on his ass, and I almost fell, but I got back in position and tried to catch up. Several of us started breathing hard—I hoped from laughter and not because they were wimping out.

At some point, after about a minute, the moves we had to copy were becoming more and more, well, feminine.

The staff sergeant next to me stopped when we had to do a limp wrist flick, saying "No, no. That's enough."

He stepped back, drawing a chorus of boos. Each move got more and more effeminate, and the crowd, especially the WM's, thought this was hilarious. All 12 of us were pretty solid guys, and it was now clear that we'd been picked for a reason. Twelve big, muscular Marines, prancing around like tinkerbells behind two slim cheerleaders was pretty funny. I almost stopped, though, my in-the-closet programing ready to kick in, but then I thought, why the hell not? Maybe it was the messed-up thoughts in my head since Taylor had told me that story, or maybe it was just in keeping with my hide in plain sight tactic, but I decided I was going to be the gayest guy on the stage.

I camped it up into high gear, swaying my hips and being more feminine than either of Kelsey or Keela. I've never been much of a prancing pony-type, but boy, did I pour it on, swaying my hips, flipping my wrist, and with head flicks that almost broke my neck. And the crowd loved it.

But I was not alone. The biggest guy of us on the stage, a dark green Marine I didn't know, was in full camp-mode as well. Once I realized that. I moved over to cut him off. I almost lost it when he showed a dramatic pique, then brushed in front of me, almost knocking me down.

"Oh, no, you don't, girl!" I shouted, even if between the laughter and the music, I doubt many heard me.

I jumped back in front of him with my own dramatic flair.

All this time, Kelsey and Keela were in front of us, leading the dance. Keela—or was it Kelsey?—turned around and saw us, with all the other guys stopped and laughing. She grabbed the other girl and then both stopped, just laughing as the two of us kept going.

To be honest, after only 30 seconds or so, I had run out of moves—like I said, I'm not too artsy. But mercifully, the music was coming to an end. I slowed down, and my opponent, sensing victory, turned to the crowd. Just before the last notes, I tackled the son-of-a-bitch and sat on his back as the music stopped.

He lay still for a moment, then started shuddering. I started to get concerned; like I said, he was a pretty big guy. But then I realized he was laughing. I got off of him and helped him up. Hand in hand, we both curtseyed, then held out our cheeks for Keela and Kelsey to kiss.

I left the stage, sashaying back to my seat, but not before three different WM's reached out to grab my ass as I went by.

Sexual harassment!

"You are such a fag, Alex," B-man said as I sat back down.

"You're just jealous you don't have the moves," I said, fist-bumping Doc as the rest of the cheerleaders, who had changed into new costumes backstage, trotted out.

I was breathing hard, but I felt good. I think I would have made the drag queens back at Hamburger Mary's proud!

Chapter 10: Risk

My name's Ken,
and I like men,

I sat in the 5-ton, getting a lift to our next mission.

but the people at Mattel,
home that I call hell,
are somewhat bothered
by my queer proclivities.

I had my M16A4 between my legs, muzzle down, and I beat time on the stock. It was the day after the Denver Broncos Cheerleader show, and I was feeling good. I'd banished Taylor's story from my mind, the day was still hot but bearable, and I was going out with my buds on a mission. Some of the muj that had fled to Ramadi were trickling back, and we were going out in force to remind them that could be hazardous to their health.

I almost sang the next part aloud:

It's safe to say that they are really pissed at me.
They always stick me
with Barbie,
but I want them to know,
I'd prefer GI Joe,
but any able-bodied man doll would surely do
for someone to love since I am not set up to screw.

I doubt any of my fellow Marines had ever heard of *The Negro Problem*, the name for this singer and writer from LA, Mark "Stew" Stewart, but after hearing him on NPR one night in the car, he became my favorite singer, with "Ken" my all-time favorite song.

"Ken" was my cruising name when I hit the town on the weekend, my tribute to the both the song and to the six-pack, dickless doll who graced little girls' rooms around the world.

Across the bed of the 5-ton opposite from me, B-Man nudged Rhymer, one of his lance corporals, and pointed at me as I slapped my weapon to the beat of the music in my head. I gave him a thumbs up, exaggerating my head movement, mouthing the words, and he laughed.

B-Man was a good guy, my brother in arms, but I wondered what he'd say if he knew what I was singing—and how the song affected me. He might be OK with it, but you never knew about that kind of thing.

I automatically looked up to the front of the truck bed where Sergeant Les Fullerton sat. The sergeant was the Third Squad leader, but more pertinent to me and my career in the Corps, he might know I'm gay. It had been bad luck, really, but maybe I should have been paying more attention to my surroundings.

Hillcrest was a good hour south of Pendleton, maybe more, with lots of places to go between the two. Most guys hung out in Oceanside or Carlsbad when they went out—you didn't have to drive all the way to San Diego to drink a beer or catch a movie. I'd always seen military guys in Hillcrest, most being Navy, but a few Marines, probably from the Recruit Depot, Miramar, or Pendleton (or like the Vulture, all the way from Yuma), but I had never seen anyone I knew until one Saturday night when I was dressed to kill and cruising. I was outside, one of the bars, leaning in, one hand holding me off the wall while pressing my point to a slender Asian guy who was back up against the building as he considered my proposition.

"Hey, Corporal Indigo!" a voice called out.

I looked up to see Sergeant Fullerton with his wife, stepping out of the next-door Thai restaurant.

I immediately pushed back off the wall. I could feel my face turn red, and I knew I looked guilty as hell—which pissed me off that I'd even feel that way.

"Oh, Sergeant Fullerton. Out for Thai?" I asked ignoring the obvious.

"Yeah, this is our favorite Thai restaurant. We used to come here all the time when I was on the drill field. Uh, have you met my wife? This is Nok."

His wife took my hand, and with an Asian accent, said, "Please to meet you, corporal."

"Me, too. I mean, please to meet you. I'm Alex."

I could almost feel the guy next to me stiffen. I'd already told him I was "Ken."

"Nok is Thai, and this is the best place for authentic Thai food, if you like that," the sergeant continued before looking expectantly at the guy I was hitting on.

"Uh . . . this is . . ." I started, realizing I didn't even know the guy's name. "This is Chang, a friend of mine," I said, pulling the first name that came to my head and immediately knowing I'd fucked up.

The look on both the sergeant and his wife's face told me they didn't believe that for a second, and the guy stood up straighter.

"Oh, well, hi. Good to meet you, uh, yeah. Good to meet you," he said, not even trying to use the bullshit name. "Well, we're on the meter, so we need to get to our car. Have a good night."

Hillcrest, dressed the way I was, outside hitting on a guy who was far more obvious in his gender proclivities than I was—well, it didn't take an Einstein to figure things out.

As soon as the two started making their way down the sidewalk, the guy stood up and pushed me in the chest.

"Chang? Chang? You fucking rice queens are pathetic," the guy said. "I'm American, and not even Chinese. I'm a fucking Filipino, and my name's Greg, not that you bothered to ask."

I'm not really a rice queen; I like what I like, and that's not based on race. I'm more of an equal opportunity lover. But I knew I was in the wrong, and I didn't bother to protest.

"So . . . you . . . can . . . take . . . a . . . fucking . . . hike!" he said, punching my chest with a forefinger at every word.

He brushed by me and went back into the bar. I was tempted to follow, but I ended up turning around and leaving, knowing this night was shot.

Sergeant Fullerton had never mentioned the incident, but he had to know I was gay. We'd worked together, hell, we'd played together on the B-ball court and in more than a few card games, and as far as I could tell, he never treated me differently than he treated anyone else.

Which was how it should be, I thought. We interacted as Marines, not as potential lovers. It was no different than male and female Marines working together.

The truck slowed, then stopped with a lurch, interrupting my thoughts. We clambered out as the platoon sergeant started shouting orders and we got ourselves situated in formation. Our mission today was an easy one. We'd spend the day checking various buildings, trying to find bomb-making factories or caches of weapons. Two IEDs had gone off yesterday, one of them destroying a hummer and wounding a Marine. The second had detonated under an MRAP, the trucks developed to counter IEDs, causing no damage. Someone was making the bombs, and the entire company was outside the wire today, putting the pressure on the muj.

We were the assault force, acting like beaters as we moved through our target neighborhood. Second Platoon was off several blocks to our right, while Third was up ahead, acting as a blocking force. If the muj started to run from us, Third would scoop them up.

Our squad moved down a block, then turned on line with the rest of the platoon. We would sweep up the left side of our formation, providing flank security. Sergeant Jackson radioed the lieutenant, then getting his OK, he motioned us forward.

The squad was in a staggered column, Ben's team on point on the right side of the street, my team next on the left, and B-Man pulling up the rear back on the right. Within the confines of the built-up area, this gave us the most mutual support.

I had my 203 loaded with an HEDP round, which could penetrate 2 inches of steel—or more of a normal haji building's wall—then explode with an ECR, or effective casualty radius, of five meters. If we went into a building, I'd switch to the buckshot round.

We started slowly moving up the street, keeping abreast of the other two squads. The intent was never to be out of range of each other for mutual support. We'd only advanced 150 meters before our first halt. On the next street over, Sergeant Fullerton's Third Squad had entered the first flagged building. With us on the back side of the block, we were now a blocking force in case any muj fled our way. We stayed put, both watching to the right for the fleeing rats and watching to our left to make sure no one came at us from that direction. We didn't hear any firing, and after 20 minutes, Sergeant Jackson got us to our feet, giving us the kill sign. We knew the building had been empty.

That wasn't a surprise. Sometimes, the so-called cooperatives were plants, sending us out on wild goose chases, spreading our manpower too thin to find the actual bad guys. Sometime the cooperatives were right, but the bad guys moved out in the meantime. Sometimes, I think the cooperatives were just fishing, telling us anything so they could take credit, and the money, if we actually hit on something.

We got back on the move, advancing slowly, searching for any signs of activity. Fallujah was a big city of almost 300,000 people, and it just didn't stop when we were around. People had to work, to shop, to get on with their life. We may be on patrol, weapons ready, but kids played soccer in the street while we passed and people went to buy food or conduct business. It made it easy for a potential bad guy, especially a suicide muj, to get close to us, so we had to note and evaluate every person on the street. At the moment, five young boys, each around nine or ten years old, were pacing Ben's team, probably asking for candy or sports gear. They'd do better asking the CAG guys—part of their job was to give out soccer balls and the like. We grunts might have a bit of pogey bait, but we didn't carry larger items just to give away.

Some guys liked having the hajis around. They thought they were like canaries in the mines: they would give us warning if we were about to hit.

Not always.

I was watching the boys, who were laughing and joking, when a blast took out half of the building beside Ben's team, showering them with rubble.

I got down to a knee, scanning for an enemy, when shots rang out. A city street does not offer much in the way of cover, but there is always something. I dashed ahead to a gateway into a courtyard, using the six inches of concrete post to give me a little cover while I tried to acquire a target.

"Doc up!" someone called from the other side of the street.

I took a quick glance. Three dust-covered Marines were getting to their feet from the rubble. Another two were down, but I could see Sergeant Jackson, who'd been moving with Third team, struggling to sit up. Just a few meters from him, out in the middle of the road, two of the boys were motionless, face down. The blood pouring from one crushed head looked inordinately bright in the tan dust.

Rounds pinged in the street.

"Where's it coming from?" I shouted out.

"Up ahead, 50 meters, second floor, above the black awning!" I heard Whitman shout back.

I saw the building, but because it was on my side of the street, I didn't have the angle.

"Cover me!" I shouted, and as weapons opened up, especially the sweet song of Chester's SAW, as I dashed across the street, almost jumping the dead boy before taking cover behind some of the rubble. I saw the muzzle of an AK47 as it spit rounds back at us.

"You waited too long, mother fucker," I said as I brought up my rifle. Fifty meters was nothing to the attached grenade launcher, and within seconds, I had flipped up the M203 sight and aimed at the window. I didn't even have to hit it; the HEDP round would go right through the concrete wall.

I pulled the trigger, and as soon as I saw the 40mm grenade start on its trajectory, I knew it was a hit. I switched to the M16 and fired off a round as the AK jerked back just before the grenade flew through the window. I hoped the mother fucker had seen his death coming and knew he was on his way to hell. An instant later, the explosion lit up the room, fire and smoke blasting out of the window.

"Get some, corporal!" Chester shouted from behind me.

We were still receiving fire, and I popped in another 40 mike-mike, looking for another target. Doc was with the sergeant, who was pushing him away to take care of the other downed Marine. They were all covered with so much dust that I couldn't tell who was down and who was fighting.

It had only been a minute since the initial blast, which was nothing in a firefight, but if the muj were going to try and run, it was getting to be that time. And I didn't want anyone to get away.

"You OK?" I asked Sergeant Jackson.

"Yeah, I'm fine," he said, sounding anything but fine. "Third Squads on it's way."

That would be too late, if the muj ran, and we were still taking fire.

"I'm hitting them," I told my squad leader, who nodded back.

"B-Man, on me," I shouted, turning to see him raise a thumbs up from where he was crouched alongside a building. "Third, base of fire! First, go!"

Immediately, Chester, Sung, and Jessie jumped up and charge forward, joining me as I sprinted back across the street and 10 or 15 meters ahead. A shape moved in the corner of my eye, and I swung my M16 around to blast it when I realized it was a woman dashing out of a doorway and back to the rubble of the fallen wall, screaming piteously. Women could be suicide bombers, but her anguish was so real that I put her out of my mind. The four of us took knees while B-Man's team rushed forward, passing us and advancing another ten meters.

I snapped off a shot at a black-clad figure with the unmistakable outline of an AK on a roof just ahead. I don't know if I hit him, but I sure made him pull back. We kept firing and moving forward.

Something hit my helmet with a snap, driving the forward edge back. I brought my hand up, not sure if I was hit, but there was no blood. My team got up and rushed forward again, coming right to the edge of the building with the black awning.

"Shit, I'm hit!" Chester called out.

I spun around to see him sink to his ass, both hands grasping his right thigh.

"Go, go!" he shouted. "I'll be OK."

I hesitated, yelled back, "Doc up!" waiting to see Doc Possum acknowledge me.

"Coming in from the right!" a voice shouted, and I turned back to see Marines from Third Squad pouring from out of a building.

They hadn't waited to reach the cross street but made their way through the block of buildings.

"Get that SMAW up here," I heard Sergeant Fullerton shout as a one of the attached Weapons Platoon SMAW gunners stumbled forward, his rocket ready to fire.

"Where do you want it?" Fullerton shouted out.

I was about to point, but I realized we were not taking fire. I listened for a second to confirm that. The insurgents had bugged out. I still almost asked for the SMAW gunner to fire, but we didn't know who was in that building. There could be a family huddled on the ground floor for all I knew.

"They're gone. Can you clear that building, though?" I asked, pointing. "Especially the second floor.

"You've got it. Take Doc Terry and take care of Chester," the Third Squad leader said.

I felt a relief. Along with Doc Terry, I ran back to where Chester was sitting, pale as a ghost as he put pressure on his thigh. Doc Possum had been moving forward, but with Doc Terry there, he waved and went back to Ben's team.

"You OK, Chester?" I asked as Sergeant Fullerton led his squad into the building, the lieutenant, who'd just arrived, in tow.

"No. I just got fucking shot," he said, his attempt at humor falling flat with his voice so raspy and quiet.

'Let me take a look," Doc Terry said, as he knelt beside Chester.

He pried up Chester's hands, and blood rushed out before Doc applied direct pressure of his own. Chester's head went up, and he lay back onto the street. I felt faint seeing the amount of blood.

"Fucking A!" Doc Terry said. "Possum, we need a Priority 1 CAEVAC!" he shouted down the street.

"Already coming!" Doc Possum yelled back.

"Give me pressure, now!" Doc Terry told me.

I replaced his hands while he fumbled in his kit, pulling out a hemostat.

"OK, move your left hand," he told me, and as soon as I did, blood spurted up, hitting me in the chest.

Doc reached into that mess and clamped something shut.

"OK, that's good," he said. "That's the femoral."

Sung and Jesse had arrived and were standing, just watching and looking worried.

"Security, you two. Now!"

"Hey, Alex!" Chester said, still on his back.

"Yeah, buddy."

"This is like every bad war movie, but I still got to ask. Are my balls OK?"

"Yeah, they're OK. You got your codpiece on."

"I know, but can you see them? Are they OK?"

I looked at Doc, who was taking out some Celox pouches. He nodded down at Chester's crotch, so with my free hand, I ran it up above the wound and under his armor. The two balls felt fine, and there was no blood.

I figured he'd have felt my hand, but he asked, "Well, are they there?"

"Whole and fine. Awfully big for such a wimp, if you ask me."

He smiled and said, "You're just jealous of them."

That smile disappeared when Doc Terry pushed my hand away and applied the Celox pad to the wound. It wasn't supposed to hurt, but no one told Chester that, and he screamed out in pain.

"Hold this in place," Doc told me.

"For how long?"

"About five minutes, but don't let go until I tell you."

He gave Chester a total evaluation, but evidently, there was only the shot to the leg. There was an awful lot of blood on the street, but Chester was still with us, and most of the bleeding had been stopped. He went back to his kit and continued to work on Chester while I kept pressure on the Celox pad.

A few minutes later, I could hear the LAV coming up the street. It stopped at the rubble, where I could see them load Sergeant Jackson, two other Marines who I still couldn't tell who they were, and one of the Iraqi kids. Once they were loaded, they carefully went around the still screaming woman who was kneeling by the body of the dead boy, tearing at her clothes. She ignored the big armored vehicle.

By now, Chester was out cold, and as the LAV came up to us, I asked Doc Terry if Chester was going to make it.

"He should. He's lost a lot of blood, but I think he's got an excellent chance."

The LAV stopped beside us, and with Sung and Jessie helping, we lifted Chester up and into the LAV. Sergeant Jackson looked at us, then waved. His black skin looked like gray liver, but he was conscious.

And then I saw who the other two Marines from Third Team were. Lance Corporal Theo Montrose was on his back, Doc Possum tending to him. One arm was mangled, and there was blood coming out of his ears. I barely noticed him. On the deck plates of the LAV, Ben lay, limp and motionless. Montrose looked worse off, but there was something about Ben that rang warning signals in my mind. I looked down at him, then up at the sergeant, who simply shook his head.

"No!" I said, stepping back from the LAV as the crew chief closed the hatch.

It just wasn't possible.

Chapter 11: Heroes

Amazing Grace, how sweet the sound,
That saved a wretch like me.
I once was lost but now am found,
Was blind, but now I see.

We didn't have a real bagpiper, but the recording finished up the dirge as we stood in the chapel during the Heroes' ceremony. I'd been to more than a few of them before, but this was the first time I'd really known one of the fallen, or in this case, two of them.

I'd found out about Ben at the scene. He'd been crushed by the blown-out wall, and I'd come to grips with that reality. But I hadn't expected to be told that night that Chester hadn't made it. He'd died on the operating table.

I'd lost it when Doc Possum told us. I wanted to blame someone. Doc Terry had told me Chester would make it, so it must be his fault. I cursed him, all the time knowing who really was at fault. It was me.

I'd been the one to order the two teams forward. I put us in danger, playing the machismo Marine Corps game. I could have waited for the lieutenant and Third Squad, but no, I had to move right then with only two fire teams, so intent was I to kill the muj.

And it had all been for naught. Sergeant Fullerton had cleared the building. There had been five Iraqis inside, but they were civilians, so I'd at least been right in not using the SMAW. Upstairs, there had been plenty of blood, but also a blood trail. My 203 had found a victim, but someone else had survived to haul him away. Whether he was dead or still alive, well we didn't know, but the lieutenant was sure there had been too much blood for the guy to have been alive.

Too much blood. Fucking ironic.

That was what had killed Chester. Despite surgery, despite the transfusions, his body had just given out from blood loss. I still didn't understand it. If he made it back to the hospital, with all their modern technology, why couldn't they save him? He died from blood loss when any of us would have given our blood from him? It just didn't make sense. But in the front of the chapel, were two sets of boots, two sets of dog tags, two rifles, and two helmets perched on the butt of the rifles. It was sinking into me that both of my friends had died.

I barely listened as the chaplain gave his eulogy. I ignored the battalion commander, the sergeant major, the company commander, and the first sergeant. I did listen to B-Man talk about Ben, and I listened to Chester's best friend, a corporal from Charlie Company, tell their stories, but mostly, I just sat, staring at the helmets.

Yesterday, the two Marines, my friends, had been full of life, three young men with futures in front of them. Today, they were in body bags at Balad, waiting to go home.

This was my second combat tour, and so far, both the battalion and I had been lucky. Right here during the Battle of Fallujah, 71 Americans had been killed. We'd experienced nothing like that. And as for me, this was some big adventure, some big game. I knew the stakes were high, and the consequences could be severe, but that was always something that happened to other people, not to me, not to my friends.

Now I knew different.

Chapter 12: Denial is a River in Egypt

After the ceremony, some of us hung around, telling stories about each of our lost brothers. It was as if we were unable to let go, as if as soon as we went back to our routine, it would all become real. As long as we were joking and talking, Ben and Chester were still with us.

But there was still a war to fight, and we were slated to go out of the wire again at 0400. The company gunny came up and gently reminded us of that, and so we reluctantly broke apart.

Going out was nothing new, but there were still things that had to be done from drawing ammo and chow to attending our operations order. On occasion, we even conducted rehearsals if the lieutenant thought the mission required it. So off we went, preparing for the next patrol, for the next time we would go into harm's way. It weighed a little heavier on my mind this time, however.

At 2100, we were finished, and most of the squad racked out to catch some Z's. I couldn't sleep, though, so I went outside, simply to gather my thoughts. I really wanted to call Grandpa. He'd been infantry, and in some serious shit. He had to know what it was like. But I hesitated. Grandpa had ice in his veins, a hard-charger despite his age, and I didn't want him to think I was a pussy. Dad, well, Dad had never lost a Marine, to the best of my knowledge. I loved the man, but even if he was a Marine, we didn't have the same experiences.

I couldn't burden the rest of my squad, either. They were going through the same thoughts and feelings. I just had to deal with it myself.

I was sitting on one of the concrete benches, staring at the spread of stars in the sky, when someone said, "They told me you were out here."

Taylor stepped out of the darkness to sit beside me.

"I saw you at the ceremony, but I didn't want to butt in."

I shrugged.

"Ben, he was a good guy."

No shit.

"And, I just, well, I just wanted to give you my condolences."

I still said nothing, and for a full minute, we both just sat there in silence.

"Uh, OK I guess you want to be alone. I understand," he said, standing up.

That wasn't fair. He'd done nothing wrong and was just giving support.

"No, Taylor. I'm sorry. It's just been, well . . ."

"I know. I understand," he said, sitting back down.

"Do you believe in heaven?" I blurted out.

"Heaven? I'm not sure. But yes, I guess so."

He didn't sound positive, more like he was simply assuring me, but I let it go.

"When I look up at the stars, I have to, you know? I just hope we deserve to go there when our time is done."

"Ben was a good man. So was Lance Corporal Leister. If there is a heaven, I'm sure they'll be there."

I laughed and said, "Ben maybe. I'm not sure about Chester. 'Chester the Molester,' we called him."

That was the first time I'd laughed in two days, and it somehow broke a dam in my emotions. All the guilt I'd been holding in for ordering us forward, all the sorrow I felt, came rushing out. The tears welled up in my eyes.

Most of us had cried either when we found out or during the ceremony, but that was the slow tears that formed, only to be brushed away with our sleeves. We were Marines, and Marines got killed. We had that facade to uphold. But right here in the dark with Taylor beside me, the faucet was open, and I out-and-out bawled.

Taylor hesitated, I'm sure not knowing what to do, but finally, hesitantly, he put his arm around my shoulders, and I leaned in, head on his shoulder, as I tried to tell him how I was guilty, how I let my thirst for action get Chester killed. He kept disagreeing, telling me it wasn't my fault, but I kept insisting, whether because I really believed it or whether I just wanted him to keep reassuring me, I didn't know.

I'm not sure how long we sat like that: ten minutes, an hour, all night? But it felt good, just to be held. My tears were soaking into his utilities, and the smell of them, mixing with his accumulation of a day's sweat, created an essence that sunk deep into my synapses, welling up emotions I had suppressed since leaving Pendleton. Loneliness, anger, sorrow, attraction, all mixed together in an emotional brew. It was too much for me, and I lifted my head, put my hand in back of his neck, and pulled him in for a kiss, a long, passionate kiss, pouring my soul into it. And for a glorious second, he returned it, giving and receiving . . .

. . . until he jumped back, shouting "What the fuck, Alex? What are you doing?"

I stood, reaching out for his hands, which he immediately snatched back.

"It's OK. I know."

"You know what?"

"That you're gay."

"Where did you get that idea," he said, the anger rising in his voice as he took another step back.

"Why deny it? I'm gay, too, and I can feel it."

"You are fucking high, Indigo. I'm not gay!" he shouted.

"Shhh," I said, using using my hands to indicate he needed to be quiet. "We don't need anyone else to hear."

"You should have thought of that before you tried to kiss me!"

"I didn't just try, Taylor. I did it, and you kissed me back."

"What? What? No way! Look, I'm sorry if you got the wrong idea, but I'm straight. I've always been straight."

I took a step towards him, saying, "It's OK, you don't have to pretend."

"You take one more step towards me, and I'll knock your fucking head off, you fag. Get the fuck away from me and leave me the fuck alone!"

He wheeled and almost ran off into the darkness while my mind took the gut shot.

Was I wrong? Was he really straight?

Now fear set in. If he was straight, and if he reported me, I was toast. I'd be discharged from the Corps.

But I'd felt that one second when he was kissing me. Not me kissing him, but him kissing me. I couldn't have mistaken that, could I?

Now doubts started to creep in. I'd been sure he was gay, I'd been sure that he was attracted to me. How the hell had I messed that up?

Expecting the MP's to jump out of the darkness at any moment to arrest me for attempted rape, I got up and hurried back to the squadbay. If my mind had been messed up before, I was now a frigging basket case, and we were going back out beyond the wire in just a few hours.

I am such a fucking idiot! I thought as I slunk back to join my squad.

Chapter 13: The Reveal

I kept waiting for the other shoe to drop, to get a message to see the sergeant major or the the staff judge advocate. I knew I'd blown it, me, the guy who took care to stay in the closet, the guy who didn't fuck Marines. In a moment of weakness, I'd put everything at risk. But as each day passed without a summons, I began to relax. If Taylor were going to turn me in, he would have done it.

And what happened began to get cloudy in my mind. I'd kissed him, that much I remembered clearly. But had he kissed me back? Was that reality or my raw emotions wishing he'd kissed me? His reaction had been violent, excessively so. The more I thought about it, the more I was convinced I'd screwed up. My gaydar usually was accurate, but all systems break down occasionally.

I spent the next several weeks avoiding him, picking strange hours to go to the gym, and getting take out food instead of sitting down inside, at least until I realized that he wasn't showing up either. I figured he was going to DFAC 1 now, and that was fine with me.

I just put my mind back on my job. My fire team was down to three now, something that slapped me in the face each time we went out. Sung was still the rifleman, and Jessie moved up to the SAW. We'd never trained with only a three-man team, and it took a little getting used to.

Over with Third Team, Whitman had moved up to team leader, so they had more of an adjustment. And the squad had a new squad leader. I was the senior corporal, so I could have moved up, but the skipper sent Sergeant Gutierrez, the company police sergeant, to take over. He'd been a rifle squad leader before, so I was happy to let him take the position. Right now, I just wanted to make sure I got Jessie and Sung back home in one piece.

Sergeant Jackson had asked not to be medevaced back the the States, and with the battalion surgeon's approval, he'd taken over Sergeant Gutierrez' position as police sergeant, leg cast and all. His nose was smashed, and he'd always carry the scar on his chin, but we told him it just made him look tougher.

And each day, I filled in one more open space on my short-timer's calendar. As with most of us, my calendar was a nude woman. Most of her was filled in. She still had her nipples left, and the final space would be her pussy, but most of her was visible by now. Every day, when guys would fill in one more space, they started showing their calendars around.

My calendar had been printed out, and I filled in each space with an appropriately-colored pencil, but some of the guys had real photos on their laptops. Zim's photo was of his naked wife, and he was not above showing us the progression as he clicked off each blocked space, revealing more and more of her as he chortled about how soon he'd reveal the last space.

Straight guys were fucking weird.

Inherent to getting close to to re-deployment, most of us got a little more cautious, not wanting to get someone hurt so close to going home. We were getting short-timers fever. The first sergeant gave us a lecture on that, and we all nodded and shouted "Ooh-rah!" but still, we weren't going to take big unnecessary risks.

Most of us. A few guys, anxious that they hadn't become heroes yet, pushed the envelope. Luckily, no one in my squad fit that bill. If some private wanted to hunt for a medal, he'd mostly be putting himself at risk. But if a squad leader, or worse than that, a platoon commander, were in the mindset, it would be the rest of us who suffered.

When the advance party from the next battalion arrived, we knew our time was getting close. We'd head to Kuwait for a few days to "decompress," then it was back to the US. I wasn't the only one getting anxious to get back.

So when the house call mission was handed down, I was not overjoyed. A "house call" was when we went out to some house and captured a person of interest. Normally, these happened in the middle of the night when most people were asleep. The best thing was to catch them all in bed so they were too befuddled to put up much of a fight. Given the chance, they would fight, because these were pretty important guys, and pretty important guys often had bodyguards.

To make matters worse, this was a daylight snatch. Intel wasn't sure their POI would even be there tonight, so we had to move, and we had to move now. We were ready—we'd been the MEF reaction force, which meant we were standing by, but without any major offensive operation going on, we hadn't expected much in the way of action.

We had to move fast, not allowing our target enough time to get away. That meant gun HUMVEE's and LAV's. We got our brief, then took off for the staging area. Sung, Jessie, and I found our hummer and driver, then jumped aboard. Jessie took the .50 cal in the turret, and we waited for our passenger and then to move out. With only three of us, we had room for one more, and the lieutenant told us to stand by.

For all the rush, we waited—and waited. Typical Corps: hurry up and wait. I thought maybe we had assets at the target, and the POI might have already moved. If that happened, we'd stand down, and I was fine with that. Four days and a wake-up was too short to be getting hurt.

I was in the passenger seat up front, and when the rear door behind me opened, I knew our passenger had arrived. It could be anybody, from a high-ranking observer to a CIA agent to almost anyone. I turned around to brief him . . .

. . . and stared, unable to say a word. Taylor had clambered aboard, and as he looked up and saw me, his face probably mirrored mine. If he could have gotten out, I'm sure he would of, but the order was already being passed on the hummer's radio that we were moving out.

"Uh, you know the drill, corporal. Just keep your head down, and the door closed. If anything happens, listen to me."

Which was a shitty brief, but that was about the best I could do as I swung around to look forward, feeling his eyes burn into the back of my neck.

It made sense that we had an ITT guy with us, especially for a high-value target. It was not that much of a case of bad luck that the ITT Marine would be Taylor, but it was shitty luck that he was in my hummer.

I decided to just put him out of my mind. He had his job to do, I had mine. We were just taking the same taxi to the job site.

But I couldn't. I never turned around once, but I could feel him just a meter behind me. I stewed in my thoughts, which was a bad idea. Jessie might be sticking out of the turret manning the .50, but all of us were supposed to be scanning for danger. But here I was, more concerned with someone inside the hummer with me than any muj outside of it.

The convoy left the wire, crossing over the desert sand and into the city itself. We passed the police station, the Iraqi guards waving as we drove by, heading into the heart of the city. According to the mission brief (and it had been very brief), we would be turning south once we reached Jolan and dive down the middle of

Resafa—which wasn't where our POI was located, but it would help keep our objective a secret (we hoped). Our house call was right on the border of Resafa and the Nazal, the Old City. Some of the fiercest fighting in 2004 was in the Old City, where buildings crowded together in haphazard messes around ancient squares.

"Hey, keep in trace of the hummer in front of you!" I told the driver as we drifted slightly to the left.

My mind might have been on Taylor, but I wasn't blind, and it was a bad idea to drive anywhere except exactly in the tracks of the hummer in front of us. The driver apologized, corrected, and we kept going.

I followed along with the radio as it relayed our progress. People were out and about, which tended to be a good sign—not that it had mattered when Ben and Chester had been killed. AQI—Al Qaeda in Iraq—was not above killing Iraqis, either as collateral damage or as punishment.

The lead vehicle turned off the main road and into Resafa, and the pucker-factor increased by an order of magnitude. If we were going to be hit, it would be in the dense pack of buildings. Hopefully we had sniper teams in overwatch, but it wouldn't take much for someone to toss a grenade off a roof at us, and with a little luck—good luck for them, shitty luck for us—they could get one through a gun turret and into a HUMVEE. Just last week, a grenade hit a Marine in the chest while he was in a gun turret, and he just managed to bat it away before it fell inside to explode harmlessly on the road. With split-second slower reflexes, that could have been a disaster.

We were the sixth vehicle in the convoy. We would follow in a single column until the force would split into two separate columns that we hoped would flank and encircle the objective where the assault force would enter and snatch our target. We were part of the security force, there to make sure no one came to the rescue, then to protect the route back to the police station.

Up ahead, I could see the first vehicle make the turn off Highway 10 (which wasn't much of a highway, but was the largest east-west road in the city and led to one of the bridges crossing the Euphrates) and into the warren of Resafa.

"Heads up!" I shouted, slapping Jessie's leg as he stood in the turret.

It was go-time.

We were turning off a large road onto a much smaller road, but if an M1 tank could make it down these roads, so could a HUMVEE. Our driver, a PFC whose name I'd already forgotten, started to swing wider than the first five vehicles in order to make the turn. I was just about to tell him to get back in the track of the other vehicles when something hit me hard in the ass, and we were flying in a universe of flames, noise, and smoke.

"Jessie!" I shouted out, who was half in and half out of the hummer, and as such, more vulnerable.

We were in the air for far, far too long, impossibly long, when we came back to earth with a thudding jolt, almost on the hummer's side. I'd reached for the door to brace myself, but it popped off, taking me with it to slam onto the side of the road. A body landed next to me.

The HUMVEE stood on its side for a long second, hanging above me. A hummer is our smallest vehicle. Several Marines could lift one off of a trapped comrade, if it came to that. But it was more than big enough to crush a Marine like an ant if it came down on him. I couldn't tell which way the vehicle was going to come down as it tottered there as if unable to make up its mind. I wasn't going to wait. I grabbed the collar of the Marine next to me and dragged both of us out of the way just as the hummer crashed down, bouncing on its wheels.

We started taking fire from the surrounding buildings as I dragged Taylor, I realized it was, to the side of the road and into a sunken depression, throwing him in and jumping on top. I took a quick look back to see Jessie, somehow still in the turret, jack his .50 cal around and start spraying while Sung and the driver got out of the other side.

The hummer was toast. It wasn't going to drive again, I knew. But luckily, this was an up-armored vehicle, and the armor had done its job. We were all alive. The first HUMVEE's in theater after the invasion wouldn't have been able to protect us, but this one did.

I could feel Taylor squirm underneath me, but I was looking for a target. My ears were ringing from the explosion, and the weapon reports were echoing between the buildings, so I was having a problem locating the shooter or shooters.

Two rounds kicked up the road right in front of me, and I instinctively ducked lower, pushing down on Taylor deeper into what was essentially a pothole.

Thank God for shitty road maintenance, I thought.

This pothole was the only thing giving us cover.

"What's happening?" Taylor said from on his back beneath me.

"Stay down," I answered. He'd lost his M4 in the IED explosion, so he couldn't do much. The pothole wasn't big—I was still mostly exposed, but between the pothole and me lying on him, he was pretty protected.

Jessie was firing away like John Wayne, and from behind us, more .50 cals opened up, along with the beautiful burp-burp of a mounted Forty-Mike-Mike, the Mk-19 grenade launcher, an automatic version of my M203.

There was one more flurry of incoming before it all stopped. We kept firing until the "Cease fire" call was made. Whoever was shooting at us was either dead or had decided that discretion was the better part of valor. For fighters who thought nothing of sending suicide bombers into crowded markets, they sure tended to run away in a firefight.

I shifted my weight and asked, "You OK, Taylor?"

"Just get off me," he said, panic in his voice.

"Relax. It's over."

"Get off!"

I slid to the side, his body armor poking at me. I caught on something on him, and he grunted and squirmed away.

"You OK?" I asked again, wondering if he'd been hurt.

Only I hadn't hung up on his body armor. Like some Marines, he'd slid off his codpiece while in the back of the hummer as it tended to dig into the balls while sitting scrunched up on the seats. So the SAPI plates in his body armor ended right at the hips. Below that was nothing, just standard desert digis. What I'd hung up on was a large, magnificent, hard-on.

"What the fuck?" I asked, staring at the bulge that made a tent—a very large tent—in his crotch.

"Don't look!" he wailed.

"You . . . what . . ." I started to say, then stopped, not knowing how to proceed.

"Just get away!" he said, hands on his crotch and he rolled belly down.

Getting a hard-on in combat was not normal, but it wasn't unheard of. More than a few guys have said it sometimes happens to them in the excitement of a battle. The rush of danger does things to the body, and then surviving the fight added more to the mix of hormones, and that is one of the possible manifestations of it.

But Taylor wasn't fighting. He was just on the ground, probably dazed from the IED like I was, with me on top of—"

Fucking A, I knew it! I wasn't wrong.

Dazed, the excitement of the fight, the fear of danger, realizing that he was still alive, but most of all, the body of one Corporal Alex Indigo, USMC, lying on him, *protecting* him, had evoked a reaction he couldn't hide. As weird as it might seem to someone who's never been in combat, he'd gotten a raging erection.

"Hey, you two OK?" Jessie asked from the turret.

"Yeah, just the wind knocked out of us. Give us a second."

"Do you need the Doc?"

"No. We're fine."

"Think of something else," I told Taylor. "They'll be here in a sec."

Sergeant Gutierrez was the first one to reach us, rushing up to Sung and the driver first, then around the wrecked hummer to us.

"You OK? You OK, Alex?"

"Fine. My ass is sore as shit," I said, only realizing at that moment it was true.

I was going to be hurtin' for certain for awhile, and probably with a black and blue ass as well. But it was better than getting my head crushed by the falling HUMVEE. *Our* heads, I corrected, looking over at Taylor.

"He OK?" the sergeant asked.

"Yeah. Just got the wind knocked out of him."

"I'd better get Doc to look at him."

The lieutenant came to check up on us, and I assure him that we were all fine. Doc was checking out a now-sitting Taylor, and I could see his woodie was gone.

Without a vehicle, we were out of the operation, but the mission was still on. The four of us loaded up on an LAV that came to get us, and the rest of force continued. The blast might have alerted our target, but we wouldn't know until we went and found out.

Jessie was riding high, adrenaline flowing as he fist-bumped all of us inside the LAV, telling us excitedly how he tore into the building from where we were taking fire. The LAV lurched into motion, and I gasped as pain shot up my ass. I didn't care, though.

I was excited, too, but for other reasons. I kept staring at Taylor, who refused to meet my eyes. I wasn't going to let him off that easily. He and I were going to have a long talk.

Chapter 14: Confrontation

I sat in the USO, looking at my watch. He was late—or he wasn't going to show, I had to admit to myself.

I never did see Taylor again back at Fallujah. I had one day of bedrest, lying on my stomach and ass up in my rack, which opened me up to more ribbing that you can imagine—and as usual, most of it gay-related, all coming from the straight Marines. The more I experience, the more I think all straight guys have a touch of the gay in them.

I was supposed to be rack-bound for three days, but I was going stir-crazy, so I downed the pills the Navy doctor at the hospital gave me and got up to help the mount-out. I'm not sure how much good I was doing as I was flying pretty high on the pills, but it was the effort, right?

I tried to track Taylor down, but either he was skillfully avoiding me, or there were just too many bodies arriving and leaving MEK. Before we knew it, Zim was gleefully showing us his completed short-timers' calendar with his wife's shaved pussy, and we were on the buses for Taquaddum first for a day, then on a C130 to Kuwait and Camp Victory.

At Camp Victory, we had to listen to chaplains and psychiatrists tell us about PTSD and not to beat our wives and girlfriends, and we had to fill out a form to tell them if we killed anyone, had a close friend die, or had seen dead bodies. I just wrote no to all of them. We got briefs on going back, and we had not one, but three inspections to make sure we weren't smuggling back an RPG or something. Mostly, though, we were there to relax and stand down. They didn't tell us that, but it was common knowledge. After pumping us up to be super-warriors in defense of the country, they wanted us to calm down into meek and mild citizens who wouldn't upset the civilians back home with our crass manners.

Camp Victory was in northern Kuwait, far from anything. We couldn't go out, but at least they had a Subway, a Hardees, a Pizza Hut, even a Baskin-Robbins. The chow was pretty good, but with tastes of home right there, most of us were happy to pay to eat it.

There was a large internet cafe, a big gym, and a USO with a good-sized library.

On my second day there, standing in line at the Baskin-Robbins, I saw a familiar figure.

"You just get in?" I asked Taylor, who jumped when he saw me.

"Uh, yes, at zero-dark-thirty this morning."

"So, how're you doing?"

He'd had a slightly perforated ear-drum from the IED, but other than that, he hadn't been hurt in the blast.

He pointed to his ear, then said, "Still ringing, but it could have been worse."

Yeah, you could have been crushed by the hummer, I thought, leaving that point unvoiced.

"We need to talk," I said as the line moved forward.

"I . . . I don't think so. We're cool."

"No, we need to talk. You owe me that."

His brows furrowed. I knew that was a low blow. I'd saved his life, and now I was calling in the chit?

"What time's your PTSD brief?"

The briefing tent only held about 150 at a time, so they rotated incoming groups through.

"1500."

"Meet me at 1400 in the USO."

"I don't know . . ."

"Just be there," I said, wheeling away and walking off. I didn't get my ice cream, but this was more important.

And here I was. It was 1410, and he hadn't shown up. That pissed me off, to be honest. The guy had lied to my face, I had probably saved his life, and he couldn't even talk to me man-to-man?

Fuck him, I thought. *I'll give him five more minutes; then I'm done with him.*

It was only two more minutes before a nervous-looking Taylor walked in the door. The USO was almost empty. There were the volunteer worker and a few people reading. It would get crowded later, but for now, it would do. Taylor looked around, saw me sitting in the back, and slowly made his way to me.

"Hey," he said, hands crumpling and uncrumpling his cover.

"Sit down."

He looked around the USO, took a deep breath, and then sat across the small table from me.

"Look, Alex, no matter what else, no matter about, well, you know, I want to thank you for saving my ass. I saw the HUMVEE about to fall over on us, but I just couldn't get out of the way. So, thanks."

I didn't tell him to come here to thank me, so I just sat there, saying nothing. He was visibly flustered, and he started to say something twice before shutting his mouth and just sitting, staring at the table-top between us. We sat there, two lumps on a log for almost a minute; I know because I was counting off the seconds.

"So, what do you want me to say?" he asked, scowling at me.

"I'd like you to explain," I said, giving him no slack.

"Explain what? I've got nothing to explain."

I had wanted him to come clean. I didn't want to lead him, but that set me over the edge.

Keeping my voice down, but with as much intensity as I could manage, I said, "Nothing to explain? Well, how about this? You swore up and down that you aren't gay. You screamed that at me. But when I'm lying on top of you, you have a boner as hard as steel. You don't think you should explain that?"

"Things happen during stressful situations," he said, at least not trying to lie about having a hard-on. "They can't be controlled."

He said it so lamely that I knew even he didn't believe what BS he was dishing out.

"So, what, bullets are flying, I'm on top of you, and you were imaging being in bed with Charlize Theron?"

"No, it was just the stress. I looked it up online."

And suddenly it dawned on me. Taylor wasn't lying to me. He was lying to himself. He had to know he was gay, but he couldn't admit it.

My anger washed away like a wave receding on the beach. I felt sorry for him. It was pretty obvious that he was being torn up with it. Part of me wanted to get up and leave. I didn't have time to hand-hold a virgin, especially one who wouldn't accept who he was. But I liked him—I really liked him. And at that moment, I just wanted to take him into my arms and hold him, not for sex, but just for comfort. I guess even a bull fag like me has some mothering instinct in him.

He refused to meet my eyes, so I sat for a moment, trying to plot a new course. I'd intended on just calling him out, then leaving. But he was a lost puppy, and you can't kick a puppy.

"Look, Taylor," I said, my voice calm and neutral. "There's nothing wrong with being gay. It's who we are, neither good or bad."

"I'm not gay," he said quietly and without conviction. "I'm straight."

"Have you ever fucked a woman?"

"Well, no. Not yet. I'm saving myself for marriage."

Yeah, right. I don't believe that, and I know you don't believe that.

"OK, have you ever wanted to fuck a woman?"

He was quiet for a long time, and I wondered if he was going to answer, when almost a whisper, he said, "No."

OK, here's the split in the road. It's up to him now.

"And, have you ever been attracted to a man?"

He leaned back, face to the ceiling, eyes closed. I could almost see his thoughts warring with each other.

"Yes," he finally admitted.

I felt a surge of victory. I wasn't particularly empathetic. Oh, I wasn't an asshole bitch with my hook-ups. For me, they were mostly just mutual fun. But for me to get that admission from him gave me a feeling of power—not power to abuse, but as hokey as it might sound, power for good.

I'd never been in a real relationship before, one that went above and beyond the physical. I'd had friends, and I'd had a few casual relationships like with the Vulture (which he'd smashed), but I wondered if they were more like this, where simply talking could bring forth emotions other than horniness.

"Taylor, there's nothing wrong with that. There is nothing to be ashamed of."

"I know. It's just that . . ."

"It's just what?"

"I can't be gay. It's not allowed."

Not allowed? I hadn't expected that response, so maybe I wasn't as newly empathetic as I'd thought.

"What do you mean?"

"I haven't told you this, but you know Brigadier General Redding?"

"No, I don't hang out with too many generals. So, what . . . oh, fuck. Redding? As in . . ."

"As in my father."

Ba-boom! The other shoe dropped.

"And that's why you want to be an officer, and you haven't told him."

Taylor nodded.

"Will he care?"

"Oh, yes, he'll care," he said, a wry smile on his face—wry but sad. "I'm the youngest of three. My brother is a first lieutenant, my sister is a second lieutenant, a Naval Academy grad. I'm already the black sheep by enlisting and going my way. I even had an appointment to the Academy, and I turned it down."

The Naval Academy was a full ride and ended up with a commission, so I wasn't sure why anyone would turn it down. Then I realized that the conflict within him kept him away. He wasn't sure he could handle the confined living of Academy life. Far better was to go to a civilian school in more liberal California and get his toes wet as a reservist—until he got recalled to come to the Sandbox.

"You know, maybe he wouldn't care. You're his son, after all."

"You don't know him. He'd care all right."

"I'm a Marine brat, too. My grandfather was a sergeant major, and my dad was a master guns."

"Oh, so you know what I mean."

"Uh, no. What I was going to tell you was that my dad knows. And he's fine with it."

That seemed to stun him.

"He knows?" he asked, his voice incredulous.

"Yes, he knows."

"And he doesn't care?"

"I'm not saying that. He also knows that it's a risk to my career as a Marine, but he still supports me."

That seemed to stun him, and he sat back, contemplating what I'd just said.

"I'm amazed, to be honest. But I don't think—no, I know—that my father would never accept it. He'd probably turn me in."

I felt sorry for him right then. I know many LGBT people are shunned by their family, and I knew I was blessed to have my family.

"And would that be such a big thing?" I asked. "I mean, being turned in."

"Yes," he said with a surprisingly fervent tone of voice. "I really want to be a Marine. And that's why I can't be gay. I want to be an infantry officer, like my dad, like my brother. It's always been my dream."

I hadn't expected that. I'd assumed that he wasn't as dedicated to the Corps as I was.

"And so you can't run the risk of being found out. I understand that. That's why I don't date Marines, you know."

Was that relief or disappointment in his eyes I just saw?

"I . . . still don't know if I am gay. Maybe I'm asexual."

"Taylor, you said you've been attracted to men. You are not asexual. And, well, you showed that after the IED, too."

He looked embarrassed, so I let him off the hook on his hard-on.

"When was the first time you remember being attracted to a man?"

"I don't know. When I was a teenager, I guess. That wrester, the Hawaiian guy."

"The Ro—"

"Yeah, him," he said, cutting me off, embarrassed again.

Interesting. So, he likes jocks, I thought.

"Any others?" I asked.

"A few, here and there. I kept denying it, though. I'm still not sure, in fact."

"It's OK. Nothing wrong with it. So just a few. And you never spoke to anyone about this?"

"No."

He was literally squirming in his seat. I knew I should back off and let him digest what he'd just done. Coming out, even to one person, could be traumatic to some people.

"And you," he added in a rush.

"What?"

"You," he said quieter, as if regretting it.

I felt a warm rush come over me. I'd thought he liked me, and our kiss proved it to me, even if for only a second, but to hear it, especially when he was vulnerable like this, moved me.

He was looking at me, almost dreading my response. He shouldn't have been concerned. I was the one who'd kissed him, after all. And a sense of purpose came over me, and I was going to break my cardinal rule.

"I said I didn't date Marines, but that was because I never met one who I admired, respected, and appreciated. I never said I wouldn't.

"You've got to get to your PTSD brief. Go take care of business. At 2200, meet me back behind the Hardees."

Hope, despair, excitement, and panic flooded his face.

He pulled back, however, saying, "I don't think . . . I'm not ready . . ."

I wanted to reach over and take his hand, but I couldn't do that in public.

Instead, I just said, "You don't have to be ready for anything. We don't have to do anything. I'm not going to push you at all. Just meet me, OK?"

"Just meet? No, you know . . ."

"Just meet. Whatever happens, or doesn't happen, is fine."

I waited, suddenly nervous. What I was proposing was stupid, but it was damned exciting, too. And it just felt right.

"Umm . . . uh . . . 2200? I'll try, Alex. I've got to go, now," he said, suddenly standing up. "And thanks."

I watched him leave, then sat there in the chair, wondering what I'd just gotten myself into. I've done some dumb things before, but this had to top the list.

And I realized that I had no idea how to implement my plan. This was a large base in the middle of the desert, and fraternization was a big offense. There weren't any conjugal quarters just waiting to be checked out. I knew some guys and gals were hooking up somehow, and only a few were caught doing so. I looked at my watch. I had seven hours to plan this out.

I'd been in part of a hundred military plans during my career, but this one rested entirely on my shoulders. I had a lot to do to put it in motion, I had a lot of intel to gather. But come hell or high water, I was determined that the mission would be accomplished.

Chapter 15: Giving

I stood in back of the Hardees, nervous as a teenager on his first date. I kept looking at my watch, wondering if he'd show. Taking a small bottle of travel mouthwash, I took another swig, only my tenth, swished it, then spit it out into the sand.

I did say Hardees, right? I wondered. *Or was it Pizza Hut?*

I've never been one prone to worrying about whether someone was open to my advances or not. If he wasn't, there would always be someone else who would, and life was too short to get wrapped around the axle about the guy who said no.

I almost shouted with relief when someone came around the back of the building, unbuttoning his trou, but it was someone else. It took me a moment to realize he was just taking a piss, not wanting to walk back to one of the heads.

"Hey," he said as the stream hissed onto the sand.

"Hey," I said back, not committing to anything else.

I kept expecting him to ask me what I was doing, but he finished, shook his dick a few times, then turned and walked back, not saying another word. A few moments later, Taylor came around the building, turning to look towards the front.

"Who was that?" he asked.

"Just some guy taking a piss."

"Oh, yes, I can smell it."

"So, you came."

"Yes. I did. I wasn't going to. But I came."

"I'm glad."

Shit, this is lame. Say something intelligent.

But nothing came out.

"So, what now?" Taylor asked, his voice both excited and fearful at the same time.

"I found a place where we can be alone. To talk, if you want."

"Just talk?"

I couldn't read the tone of his question.

"If you want. It's back here," I said, taking a step back.

He didn't hesitate, but followed, so I turned and led him past the transit area and over to where the permanent personnel worked on everything from getting gear ready for shipment in-country to up-armoring HUMVEE's. Behind a large motor pool, there were rows of Conex boxes. I led him down one row, stopping in front of one of the 10-foot long shipping containers. It had been re-purposed as a storage shed, filled with stacks of tires inside. I'd seen it earlier in my recon, and evidently, tires were not too pilferable because the door was partway open and unlocked. I had checked again 30 minutes ago, and it was still open, to my relief. It wasn't the most romantic place in the world, but it was the best I could do.

Once again, I asked myself what I was doing. We'd be back in the States in a few days. If anything was going to happen between us, we could do it in a clean and convenient hotel room, not out here in the sand where we both risked getting kicked out of the Corps if we were caught.

But I couldn't wait. I reached to take his hand, and then I led him into the box before I could change my mind.

And he followed.

"What do we talk ab—"

I shut him up by pulling him into me, covering his mouth with mine, and diving deep into a kiss. I tried to suck his soul out, inviting it into me. He pulled back the tiniest bit, and I was ready to hold on tight, but then he melted into me, molding his body into mine.

I'd always thought the term "melted" was too much a trope of books and movies. Guys had grabbed me, slammed into me, let me grab them, lay submissive for me, but never had anyone "melted" into my arms until now.

For ten seconds, twenty seconds—I'm not sure I was paying attention to time—he was my puppet, the object of my affection, but then suddenly, he erupted, pushing me back as his tongue shoved into my mouth. His passion almost overwhelmed me, like a physical force.

The dam had burst. He'd only the admitted the possibility that he was gay that afternoon, and he'd let me kiss him, but now he wanted to catch up for lost time. I knew he wanted to experience everything.

So much for the shy virgin.

I'm almost always the dom in a relationship. I take charge. But it was almost funny to see him like this, eager yet not quite sure of how.

Living in Altus, where everyone is a cowboy whether they had a ranch or not, I'd been around horses before, and I'd been there when they were being bred. Sometimes, with a young stallion, they were so excited, engorged and snorting around the mare, but they couldn't quite get it in. Taylor was like this.

I could feel his cock pressed against my belly, and his hand dropped to my utilities, his hand sliding down until he grabbed my cock—but too hard, jerking up on it.

Fuck, Taylor. Do you grab your own cock like that?

More to protect my cock than anything else, I spun him around so his back was up against a stack of tires and knelt. Pulling down his trou, his cock jumped up, long and hard. Only a little light made its way in the small crack in the door, but the light hit just right, a spotlight on him. And it was beautiful. Not huge, but big enough, seven inches with a gorgeous helmet, and throbbing with each pulse.

He groaned before I even touched it.

So I decided to play. Normally, I go right at it, and normally, it is me who gets pleased. I've never understood the "receptacles" who only pleasured the other guy. Sex was to get off, nothing more. But right now, I wanted to tease him, to lead him to the brink.

I traced one finger on the underside of his dick, and it almost jerked away from my touch. For a moment, I thought he was going to cum, so I squeezed his balls, applying pressure. He exhaled in a rush of air. Letting go, I licked, the gentlest, tiniest flicker right under the corona.

Taylor's groan was loud, too loud. I almost closed the door, but I wanted to see him. If we got caught, we got caught, but we were too far engaged to stop now.

Both hands reached for the side of my head, and I let him pull me in close, so my cheek was against his erection. I turned my head to give it a long, sloppy lick, from down low to up high on the glans, then swooping suddenly, engulfing the entire shaft, almost to the root. He started to pump, but I pushed against his hips, trapping his ass onto the stack of tires.

I've received more blow jobs than I've given, but I still know a thing or two. With long, slow bobs of my head, I went up and down his entire seven inches, closing my mouth tight as I cleared the head, then forcing it back through my lips, relaxing more as I went down until my nose hit his belly. Once I knew he wasn't pumping, I dropped one hand to cup his balls, massaging them as I gave him head. One of his hands dropped to the top of my head, giving me slight shoves each time I went down.

But I didn't want him to cum yet. As I felt him stiffen, I popped my mouth off of him and grabbed the base of his shaft, squeezing to stop him from reaching the point of no return.

"Oh, fuck," he said in a half-whisper, half-groan.

I pushed myself up, licking his belly, running my tongue between his pecs, up his neck, and to his mouth, flicking it in, then pulling back as he reached for it with his mouth.

"So, are you a pitcher or catcher?" I asked.

"A what?" he asked, obviously confused.

"A pitcher or a catcher," I repeated.

"I don't know what that is," he said as he thrust his hips forward, pushing his naked cock up against my erection, still under my trousers.

"Oh, you really are a newbie, aren't you? A pitcher is the one who fucks, the catcher is the one who gets fucked."

"Oh," he said, as he seemed to think about it. "I don't know. Does it . . . does it hurt? You know, to get it in the, uh . . ."

"In the ass? A little, at first, but you get used to it."

My own cock was straining against my utilities, anxious to sample his ass. His trou were down around his knees, and I cupped his ass with my hands and brought him into me hard with a powerful jerk.

"I don't know. I can try, but can you, you know . . ."

"Be gentle?"

But I didn't want to be gentle. I wanted to take him, and take him hard. But his voice, just bordering on plaintive, struck a chord with me. And I realized I was slipping into my usual, aggressive, self-centered self. That might work for a one-night stand with a sub, but I knew I wanted more than that with Taylor. I wanted something deeper.

I reached into my pocket and pulled out a condom—yes, to my surprise, the little PX had them. I bought a three-pack, sure the MP's were watching and would swoop down on me with klaxons sounding as soon as I left. But no one batted an eye. If fraternization was against the rules, then why have condoms? But I wasn't arguing.

I held it up in front of his eyes, making sure he could see it in the light that made it into the box. He gulped twice, then nodded. I took his hand, then placed it on my belt, motioning him to remove it. He trembled, but he released it, and my trou dropped, letting my own cock free. I handed him the condom, and once again, he nodded, tearing it open. He fumbled with it for a moment, trying to figure out which way it unrolled, then reached for my cock, ready to roll it on. I stopped him, and he looked up at me confused.

I took the condom out of his hand, then knelt again, to where his erection had been fading. I took him back into my mouth, and with four of five bobs of my head, he was hard again. I put the condom in my mouth, put my mouth over his glans, then slowly rolled it down over his rampant dick.

"I don't understand."

"Yes, you do, Taylor," I told him, reaching into the pocket of my trou, which were down around my ankle, rooting around until I pulled out some gun oil. They didn't have lube at the PX, so gun oil was the lube of choice in the Sandbox—or so I'd heard. I slowly squeezed out a squirt onto my hand, then ever slower, reached down to transfer it to my ass.

I swear, Taylor's eyes were about to pop out of his head. I shifted him aside, placed my hands on the tires, and bent over.

"I'm ready for you."

"Is this OK? I meant, I thought, you were going to, you know. . ."

"There'll be time for that later. This is your night."

"If you're sure, Alex. I can take it, if you want."

I looked over my shoulder at him and said, "Just do it. I want you."

He reached out with one hand and placed it on my hip. I actually shuddered, and he jumped back. I had to reach back with my right hand, grab him, and pull him into me. His cock hit me up high, almost on my back, and I had to reach down and grab it. Even through the condom, it was hot and throbbing.

For some unknown reason, I had an image of someone with a heat sensing scope, watching us through the crack in the door, and Taylor's cock burning out a brilliant white. I had to stifle my laugh.

Taylor was all excitement, but no technique. He tried pushing in, nowhere near my asshole, so I had to steer him, raising my hips to give him a better angle. I felt like ground traffic controlman, guiding in an airliner. Once I had him lined up, though, instinct took over, and he pushed forward—a little too fast for me, but not too bad. I hadn't had sex in more than seven months, and I wasn't really in fucking shape. The gun oil itself burned a bit as well.

With one hand on his hip, the other arm bent at the elbow and forearm bracing against the tires, I tried to give him a sense of rhythm. He was lost in the cloud, though, and surprising strong hands grabbed my hips, driving me back into him. I could feel his cock delve deep into me—and I enjoyed it.

Some guys can cum by getting fucked. I was never one of those, and on occasion, the experience wasn't enjoyable, depending on the partner. But this time, I could feel Taylor's rapture, and it was infectious. It spilled over onto me, into me. We were joined together, and took Taylor's hand off my hip, sliding it around to grab my own cock. He started pulling hard at it, and this time, I didn't care.

And it was over too soon. With a shudder, Taylor cried out, then squeezed me with all his might before collapsing onto my back.

Thinking back, the entire act might have taken 15 seconds, maybe 20. But a sense of peace had descended onto me, and our making love seemed timeless. The outside world didn't exist.

He lay on me, and I could feel the hot tears land on my back. The heat of the night, the smell of the smell of the tires, and his warm touch rolled together in a delicious mix of a sensual bouquet. It imprinted in my brain, never to fade away.

I heard Taylor breathing hard—or that is what I first thought. I realized he was quietly sobbing. I turned around, his cock sliding out of me hugged him. His arms went around my neck, and he buried his face in my shoulder, as spasms wracked his body.

"Shh, shh," I said. "It's OK."

"I'm sorry, I just don't know what to feel."

"Don't worry, Taylor. I understand."

And I did. Tears were a turn-off for me. But these weren't some affectation. These were real tears, tears of relief as Taylor realized just who he was.

I just stood there, holding him. Some of his tears rolled down my chest, dropping to my cock, which had started to relax after he came, but that stirred it, and it began to rise again.

Taylor must have seen that, because he reached down, gently took it in his hand, and said, "I'm ready, if you want. You can fuck me."

And I did something I've never done before. I turned him down, someone I wanted to fuck so bad.

"No, this is your night. I'll take you up on that another time, but for now, I'm fine."

And I realized I was.

Taylor relaxed, and slowly, his sobs ended. We stood there, me leaning back into the tires, him leaning into me. After twenty minutes like that, a thought struck me, and I laughed.

"What?" Taylor said, pushing away from my chest and looking at me.

"Oh, nothing, just thinking."

"No, really, what made you laugh?"

"Do you have to ask? We're here in this Conex box with stacks of tires, it's still hot as hell out there, you've still got a full condom hanging from your cock, and our trou are down around our ankles. You don't think that's funny."

He thought about it for a second, then laughed, saying, "Yes, I guess it is."

But I'd just pulled that out of my ass. That hadn't been what made me laugh.

I was just thinking about the Alex Indigo rules of sex and the military.

I guess I still don't fuck Marines. . . yet!

Chapter 16: Looking Forward

"Congratulations, son," my dad said, reaching out to shake my hand.

"Thanks."

I was still surprised he'd driven out to Pendleton for the ceremony. It has been a 20-hour drive, all for the two minutes I'd been the center of attention. There'd been nine of us in the ceremony receiving Navy Achievements or Navy Comms, and we'd been presented with them at a battalion formation. It had been heady to me, to be out in front of everyone, all of my brothers.

There were still some Bronze Stars to be awarded, and probably a Silver Star, if it got approved, but those took longer to get through the system.

I took a quick look down at my chest. The medal hung from a white and green ribbon, and in the middle of that ribbon was a gold "V." I guess officers can get the medal for making sure the general's coffee pot never ran dry, but the "V" let everyone know I'd earned it in combat.

Dad reached out and touched the "V." He had his own Navy Comms, but none with that little piece of gold-colored metal.

"And thanks for coming," I added.

"You kidding me? You think I'd miss it? My own son's medal ceremony?"

"Of course, meeting up with some of your old buddies at the SNCO Club had nothing to do with you deciding to come out, right?"

"Well, as long as I'm out here, I can't be rude, right? Wouldn't be right, doncha know."

"Right, Dad," I said, before quickly reaching out to hug him.

"Hey, PDA, son," he said with a laugh. And you're poking me with that medal."

"I love you, Dad."

"Well, I love you, too," he said. "And I'm proud of you. You're a good Marine, and you're a good son."

"Hey, congrats, Alex," Zim said, his wife on his arm.

I smiled, trying not to think of Zim's short-time calendar. I'm not sure if my face turned red, but it felt like it had.

"I hope you enjoy the Family Day," I told her. "I can smell the burgers cooking now."

"Oh, I will," she said, twining her arms around his. "It's so good to see all of you together like this."

More of my friends came up to congratulate me. I tried to brush off any idea that I'd done anything noteworthy, and compared to a few of the other awardees, that wasn't too far off from the truth.

"It looks good on you," a now-familiar voice said from behind me.

I turned and took the proffered hand.

"Thanks, Taylor," I said before turning to my father and adding, "Dad, this is Corporal Redding. I've told you about him."

"Ah, yes, you have," he said, reaching out to shake Taylor's hand. "Good to meet you, Corporal."

"It's an honor, sir."

"Sir?" my dad said with a laugh. "Don't you modern Marines say 'Don't call me sir. I work for a living' anymore?"

"Well, yes," Taylor said with a smile. "We still say that. But Alex has told me so much about you, and well, I admire you so much."

There was much more than my dad's rank to what he was saying. He was referring to my dad's acceptance of me being gay.

And my dad knew exactly what Taylor meant, but with his typical style, he averted the comment to "Eh, I just hung around so long they had to promote me. You boys, now—excuse me, you young men and women--you make me proud to have worn the uniform."

"And you paved the way for us to serve, just as your father paved the way for you, as I hope Alex, everyone else here, and I can do for the future generation."

"Oh, well said there, Corporal. You'll do fine as an officer."

"What?" Zim and B-Man asked in unison. "Redding, you're going to be an officer?"

Taylor didn't answer, but said to my dad, "If you don't mind, Master Guns, the chow line is calling, and I'd be honored to listen to a few of your seas stories while getting a few of those burgers. We can leave Alex here to bask in his glory."

"Sea stories? I guess in 30 years I have a few. And you know how all sea stories start? 'This is a no shit . . .'"

Together, the two headed off towards the Family Day chow line where people were already lined up for burgers, dogs, and whatever. Taylor had opened a Pandora's Box, and Dad had already launched into one of his many, many stories.

"What's that about Redding becoming an officer?" B-Man asked.

"Ah, nothing. That's just my dad being my dad. He likes to pull people's chains."

"Oh. OK. Anyway, congrats on the medal. You deserved it."

There were nine of us, and all the officers and SNCOs in the battalion, it seemed like, had to shake each one of our hands. Most of the Marines and corpsmen in the platoon made their way to congratulate me as well before migrating to the food.

Sung and Alicia Manuel made their way to me. Alicia had been Chester's fiancé. I'd met her three weeks ago at the memorial service for the Marines we lost during the deployment, and we had shared a few tears. Now, with the newly promoted Lance Corporal Sung, the two walked up.

"Thank you for coming, Alicia."

"It was my pleasure, Alex. I'm just down the road, and Warden came and picked me up for this."

Alicia was a local girl, living somewhere out in Vista.

"I wanted to say thank you, so I asked him if I could come."

"Thank you?"

"Yes. Warden told me you saved Chet's life, back in Iraq. I didn't know that when we talked before, and I . . . I just wanted to say thanks."

I didn't know what to say. Maybe I had saved his life back in that building. But he hadn't made it back from the Sandbox alive, so to what end?

"I'm sorry," I said, at a loss for words.

"I know. But if you hadn't done that, I would have lost all those calls, all those emails, from him. I would have lost three more months of having him."

I felt the tears well up in my eyes. I thought I'd cried myself out at the service, but deep in my heart, I knew I'd never got over Chester and Ben.

"Can I hug you?" she asked in a little girl voice.

I held out my arms, and she floated into me, head on my chest, her arms around my lower back. We stood there, holding each other, tears falling. Marines and civilians gave us space, a tiny island of our own. They had all seen this before, and they knew what we needed.

After a minute or so, she slowly pulled back. She was a short girl, so she reached to my shoulders and pulled me down, kissing me lightly on the cheek.

"God be with you, Corporal Indigo."

"Alex. I told you before, Alex."

She smiled, then turned to Sung, who put an arm around her and led her off, away from the food and towards the parking lot. I didn't know if they were forming a relationship or not. I hoped so. Everyone deserved love.

And that thought made me look up. Dad and Taylor were off to the side. I could tell that Dad was in full sea story mode, an untouched burger on his paper plate as he gestured to add emphasis on whatever he was saying. Taylor stood beside him, eyes locked in rapt attention. I don't know whether he was really that interested or if he was just doing his duty with the in-laws. Probably a bit of both.

Yes, *in-laws.*

Immediately after the memorial service, all the returning Marines and sailors had gone on post-deployment leave. Taylor and I had gone together to Hawaii, renting a beach cottage on Molokai, far from the more frenzied tourist haunts, and *experienced* each other.

We had taken a flight from John Wayne Airport in Orange County, not saying much, but hand-in-hand as we flew across the Pacific. The sexual tension had risen, and I felt I was going to explode. We had a two-hour layover in Honolulu, then the short flight to Molokai, and a longer drive to the resort. I was shaking with anticipation as we checked in as soon as we kicked out the attendant who insisted on showing us how to work the safe, the remote, and everything else in the room, we almost tore each other's close off in a frenzy of lust and passion. And it had been better than I'd ever imagined possible. Not just the physical aspect of sex—although he was an eager learner—but the entire experience.

When we came up for air a day later, I realized I was just as happy talking to him, just as happy lounging by the pool with him with a book in hand, just as happy eating with him on the lanai. Oh, we didn't give up on the sex. I was surprised by the stamina both of us exhibited. I guess the forced celibacy of the Sandbox had something to do with that for me, and a lifetime of celibacy had something to do with that for him. But we slowly gravitated from unbridled lust to something more fulfilling. We also settled into roles. In bed, I slowly assumed my normal position as the dom, but not entirely. Out of bed, he assumed the more dominant role, but not entirely. Together we were different than we were apart. And on Tuesday night, our last night before returning to California, we decided that we needed to be together--forever. It might not be legal, we might not have had a real ceremony, but on the beach, a half-moon hanging above the horizon, we made our vows to each other. In our minds, we were married, and that was more important than the opinion of any government.

We knew we would have to figure out how to proceed. Both of us were adamant about continuing our Marine Corps careers. Taylor offered to give up his goal of getting commissioned, but I wouldn't let him. Being married should open up opportunities, not hold people back. We'd just face that situation when it occurred.

And who knows? DADT was the first step, but it did not go far enough. But the world was changing, and sometime, hopefully during our careers, LGBT servicemen and women would be able to serve openly, and the law of the land would be that anyone could marry without regard to gender identity.

I watched Dad and Taylor, two men I loved very much. I was proud of my dad for accepting me, for accepting Taylor. I was proud of Taylor reaching out to my dad as all good husbands should do. I knew mom would like him, too, when we went to Altus for Christmas.

I knew I was a very lucky man.

My dad must have finished a story, his hand on Taylor's upper arm as he leaned in, and Taylor lifted his head back and laughed. My dad held onto Taylor's arm before giving it a punch and laughing as well.

The congratulatory crowd was thinning out as people went to get fed or just gather in groups to talk. Little kids ran around as little kids did. I wanted to go join Dad and Taylor, but for the minute, I just wanted to soak it all in. Soak life in.

And I realized, one more time, that in some ways, nothing had changed. In other ways, everything had. I still didn't *fuck* Marines.

But I loved—and made love—to one very, very special Marine.